THE SILENT DANCE OF STARS

Ciro Correia

www.cirocorreia.com

Print ISBN: 978-1-0369-6429-0

A DANÇA SILENCIOSA DAS ESTRELAS

希儒柯

ciro correia studio

To
Margaret J. Jameson,
brave adventurer. Gone to another
reality but not forgotten in this one.

And

Manuela Correia,
who would have disliked this story
but always loved me dearly.
I love you and miss you mum.

A sincere thank you to Heather, Anna, Mel
and Sarah for reading this book early on
and giving me encouragement.
And thank you to Elias Rowan
for his advice and thoughts.

One surprising day, the god of death did
glide across a meadow bleak but fair,
and where his feet did fall, saffron plumes
burst into a molten rage of unrelenting life
in protest at his presence there.

From the studio

Stories have always been how we explore what it means to be human.

Some ask questions about the world around us.

Others ask questions about the world within us.

The Silent Dance of Stars is one such story.

It is a work of fantasy, but its concerns are deeply human: love, memory, grief, choice and hope.

If, by the final page, you find yourself looking up at the night sky a little differently, then perhaps the story has found the place it was meant to.

Welcome.

— Ciro Correia Studio

Author's Preface

Before you begin, there are two small pieces of context that may enrich your journey.

The first concerns the tarot cards that appear throughout the novel. Their titles are presented in both Portuguese and English. This was a creative choice inspired by an early piece of research that suggested a connection between Portuguese playing cards and the later development of the tarot. Although that claim proved to be historically unfounded, the idea stayed with me. Rather than discard it, I allowed it to become part of the mythology of this fictional deck.

The second concerns the fragments entitled The Rite, which open each of the book's four parts.

They are presented as excerpts from the observations of Scarabaeus nocturnus, a rare desert beetle whose mysterious life cycle inspired one of the novel's central metaphors. The Rite itself is entirely fictional, blending natural history with myth in the same spirit as the story that follows.

Neither element is intended as historical or scientific fact. They exist to deepen the world of the novel and to invite the imagination a little further beyond the familiar.

This book has been rewritten many times over the years. Each revision has stripped away something unnecessary or uncovered something more truthful. Eventually, I reached the point every writer hopes for: not where the work is perfect, but where it feels honest enough to let go.

I hope you enjoy the journey.

A map of Abe Mendes' current reality

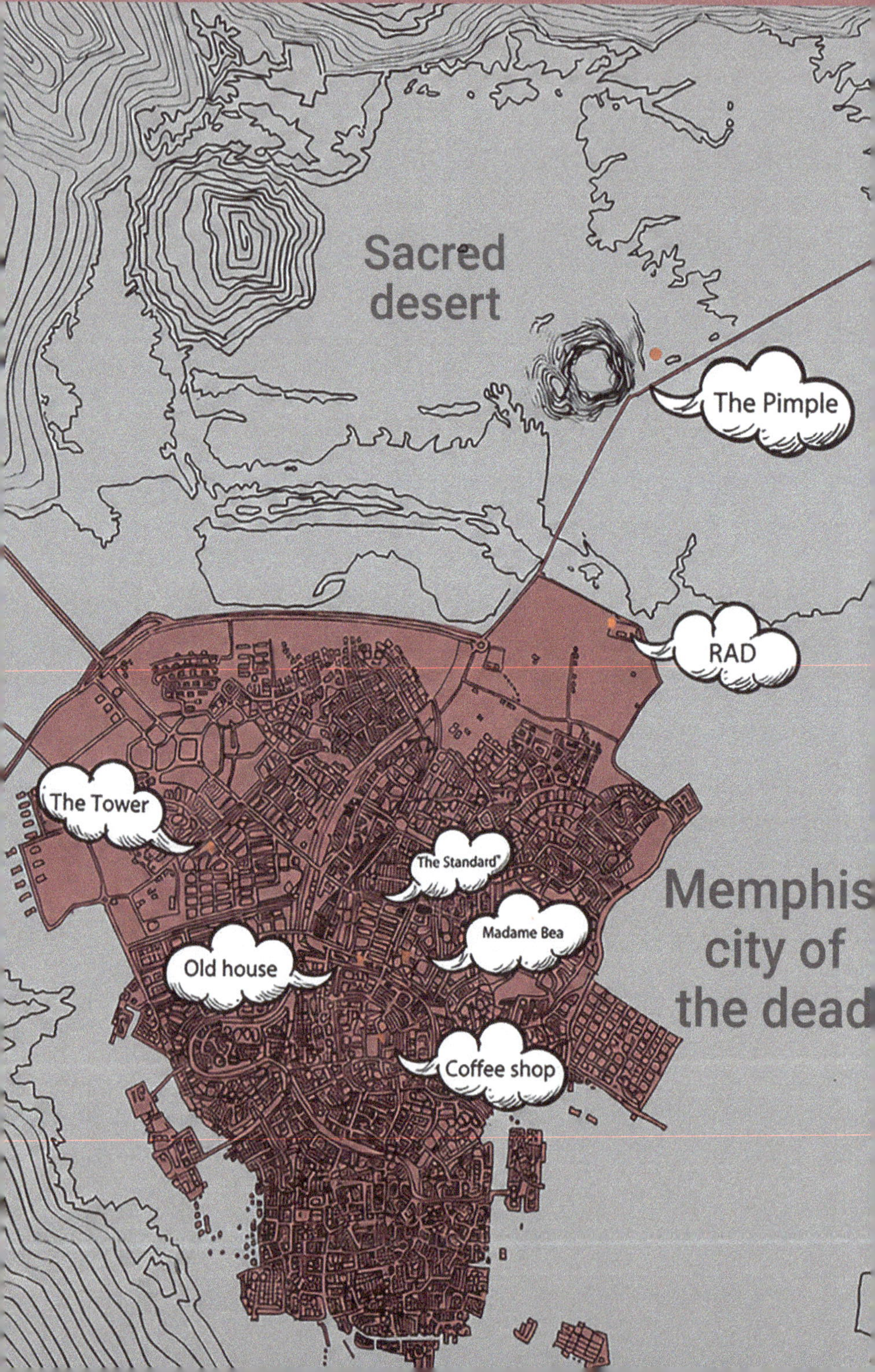

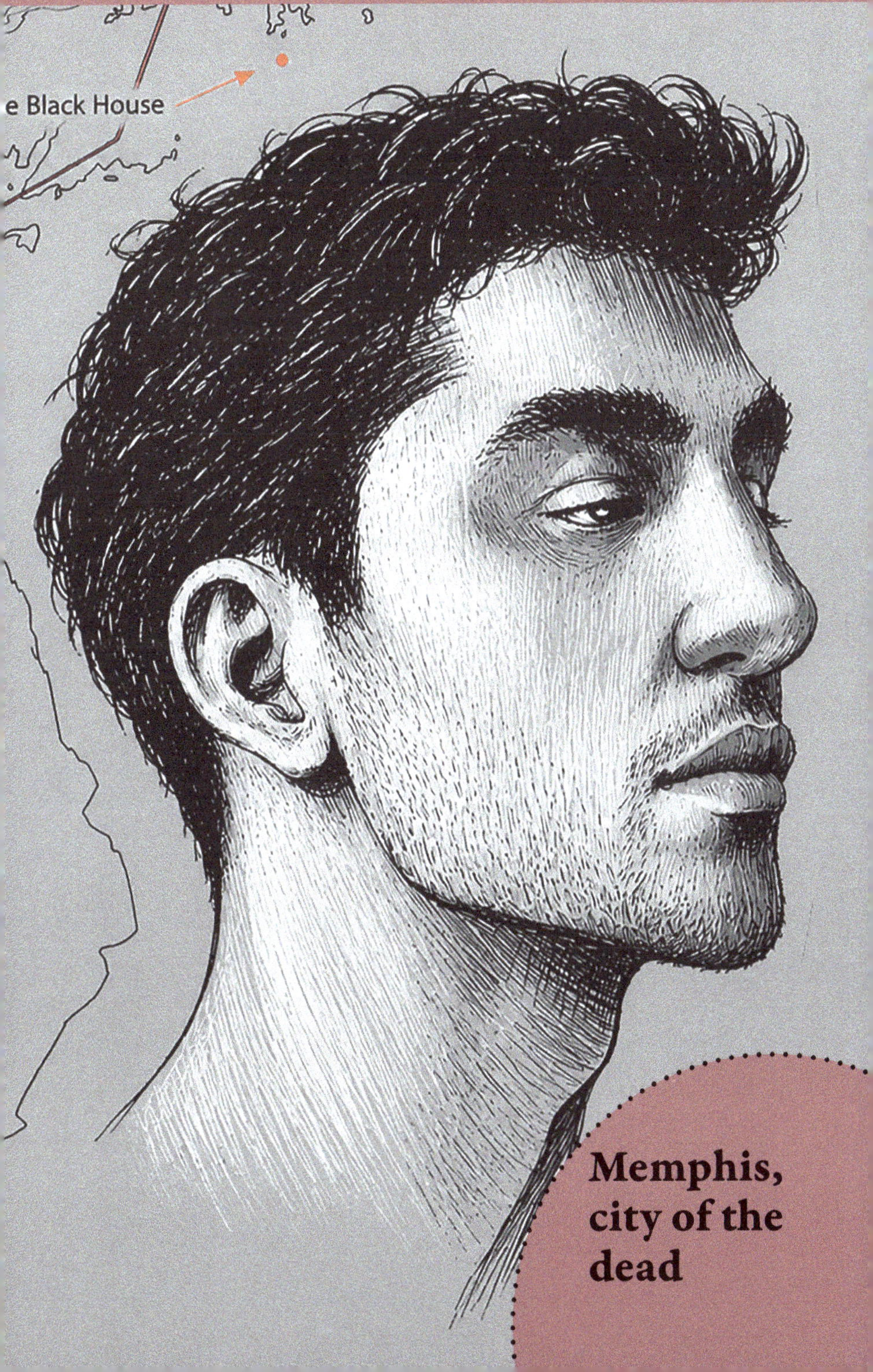

Memphis, city of the dead

CONTENTS

3

Wings of Static

Chapters

4

The Silent Dance of Stars

Chapters

40
50
♃
4 14 15 1
9 7 6 12
5 11 10 8
16 2 3 13

Part one

HUSHED LUMINESCENCE

The quiet before motion — the shimmer beneath stillness.

It begins in darkness — damp, living, hungry.

Beneath the soil, the larva shivers, feeding on rot, on memory, on itself.

Change comes like fever.

The shell splits.

Soft tissue heaves through the crack.

A body is born, slick and pale, breathing for the first time beneath an unfamiliar sky.

Jupiter

Chapter one

Júpiter

Jupiter

The desert stretched out below me, still cloaked in the bruised blue of night. Only the faintest light had begun to gather at the rim of the horizon, a slow seep of grey and silver that promised dawn but hadn't yet claimed the sky. The air was sharp and thin, carrying the scent of dust and the ghost of cold fire. I was bone-tired, hollowed and trembling from the long push into the desert, the heat, the silence, the unravelling hours without sleep. Every muscle felt borrowed, my thoughts moving like figures in fog.

Far ahead, at the base of a shallow rise, the festival

camp sprawled across the sand, a scatter of tents, vans and canopies glowing dimly beneath strings of tired lights. We'd passed them the day before, a caravan heading deeper into the emptiness, but from up here they looked almost unreal: a pocket of noise and colour still pulsing in the dark.

Even now, long after the night should have ended, they were awake. Music drifted thinly through the still air, fragmented rhythms, distant laughter, the echo of a drumbeat that didn't belong to this hour. Whatever medicine they had taken to keep the night alive still held them somewhere between waking and dream.

Beyond them, Memphis shimmered faintly at the edge of the world, its glass and steel catching the first pale hint of morning, turning the city into a mirage of fire and smoke. Then, from the camp below, tiny sparks began to rise. At first I thought they were embers from dying fires, but as they climbed higher, I saw their true form: red sky lanterns, released one by one into the paling dark.

They rose in silence, hundreds of them, trembling with small, stubborn light, slow prayers ascending into the new day. I watched as they drifted towards me on the moving air, each one a fragile star against the deep blue of twilight.

It had been more than twenty-four hours since

it began, since the world,
and everything I thought I
understood, had started to shift again.
As the first light touched the desert floor,
I felt the memory uncoil within me, pulling me
back towards the moment the veil began to tear.

She said I was still in love with someone from a previous life. It was part of my problem.

Madame Bea, clairvoyant extraordinaire, hidden between forgotten lanes within the complex inner city of Memphis, had said this to me. It wasn't anything I didn't already know. I had thought I understood love, but I knew its pain intimately. Memories of a lost lover from a past life haunted me relentlessly, a love I knew still lingered within me. The emotions surged from deep within, threatening to spill out and engulf everything around me.

I had discovered Madame Bea by accident while wandering through the dark alleys and lonely side streets downtown. I had been searching for my lost lover, hoping that, as if by magic, I would be drawn to her. I had systematically scoured the city, crossing off street after street as I went.

I now know that Madame Bea lived there, down in the murk between dilapidated buildings like some ancient spider in a web of darkness. In a lost neighbourhood once alive with vibrant tenants, now filled with untold ghost stories.

I stood in waves of rain. The lamplights down there flickered Morse-coded messages from corner to corner. The shadows played tricks on every paranoia, giving life to my worst fears.

I had been stumbling around the inner city for months before I came across Madame Bea. Like Buddha, I had awoken from the dream of existence.

It was the third year since my awakening, since my past-life memories resurfaced. That single event propelled me into searching for the ghost who inhabited my newfound mental spaces. I had searched large areas of the city within the first two years. It was illogical, I know, but I thought I might bump into her or recognise a place we had both shared. I had to do something.

In the third year, I finally turned my attention to the

claustrophobic ghettos and haunts of the vice-infested inner city. My life before the awakening was all but gone. My obsession had shattered those relationships and patterns. All I had left was a relentless desire to search for what I had once known.

I had just walked my usual circuit, stopping at the same places in a planned pattern. Part of my plan was to meet as many people as possible while scanning the crowds in the hope that somehow I would recognise her in this life. That circuit included stopping at an old cinema called The Standard.

The Standard was the only real cinema left downtown. The other cinemas and regular businesses had long since been swallowed by peep shows, porn theatres, dive bars and corner shops with more hard liquor than food. They played old classic films at The Standard to mostly empty seats. That night they had screened *Doctor Zhivago*, and I had managed to catch the last few minutes. Whenever I'm there, I always wonder how The Standard still survives. I suppose one day it won't be open anymore, and I'll walk straight past its broken Art Deco façade.

That night, instead of moving on, I walked out through the gilded doors and stood for a while studying the poster of Omar Sharif and Julie Christie. Out of the corner of my eye, something caught my attention.

A blaze of light flickered in the distance to my left. Words written in neon.

Walk this way.

So I did.

The light went out before I reached it, only to appear again farther down a side street. I crossed into the darkness, but by the time I had walked its length the light had disappeared once more. Disorientated, I tried to find my way back, but the city had shuffled its streets and I was lost.

I wove through smaller, unfamiliar side streets. In the confined blackness of the alleyways, I came upon the blaze of caustic light again, arrows buzzing, leading me deeper into its burning glow.

The cramped street folded between darkened buildings, a natural funnel towards the final destination. A large sign hung above a battered shopfront, the centre of my spiralling vision.

As soon as I saw the burning neon sign enthroned above the warped door leading into Madame Bea's narrow hole-in-the-wall shop, I knew I had to go inside and speak with her about my situation.

Pushing hard against the warped door, it jarred loose with a loud groan. It must have smacked Madame Bea's cat on the head, for the poor thing shot back into the claustrophobic space beyond the reception area with a loud screech.

Apologising to no one in particular, I cleared my throat as I stepped into the stale old air.

'Is anyone in?' I asked desperately.

Almost immediately I questioned

my sudden determination to enter Madame Bea's Clairvoya-Agency.

A short silence was followed by the rattle of footsteps descending somewhere within the bowels of the building. Someone, or something, with an enormous presence was moving towards me.

'Y-e-s! Who is it? I'm come...ing,' returned a cheery, put-on falsetto from beyond a low doorway in the far-right corner opposite the front door.

'Hi! I'm Abel... Mendes,' I called back.

The reception area was a small room with an unnaturally low ceiling. The walls were painted a radioactive green, while the wooden ceiling planks were stained a dark brown. A thick, musty woven carpet covered the floor. It was hairy, and it had set my nose on edge the moment I stepped through the front door.

Wooden benches lined the walls. Portraits of eerie-looking men and women were everywhere, arcane symbols filling the backgrounds behind them. They covered large sections of the green walls, side by side, leering at me through blackened eyes.

There were photographs of, as I would later discover, Madame Bea posing with famous celebrities, politicians and other strange-looking personalities.

In the centre of the wall opposite the entrance, a gilded frame gleamed. Within it hung a yellowed newspaper clipping.

Clairvoyant of the Year!

Naturally, I stepped closer.

Voted Clairvoyant of the Year again.

Apparently Madame Bea had held the title for several years running, decades before.

First came surprise, then genuine curiosity. I hadn't realised awards for clairvoyants even existed. How did judges decide who was the best? How did they measure something so impossible to verify?

Before I could read any further, she was standing in the low doorway.

I felt her sizing me up.

Her hair was pitch black, held back with a scarf, loose curls falling to her shoulders. Smoky grey eyes sat beneath heavy lines of dark mascara, making her look almost exotic, as though she had stepped straight from an Egyptian tomb. Her complexion was olive and, despite suspecting she was well past sixty, there were no physical signs to prove it.

Except for her presence.

Age clung to her.

Time clung to her.

She wore a tasselled rouge skirt, while her blouse shimmered with embroidered golden thread forming the shape of some great dragon across her chest. A deep purple shawl hung casually over her shoulders, and large moon-shaped earrings swung gently from her ears.

The moment she saw me, she smiled with quiet, unsettling certainty.

'Aah! I knew you would come!'

The falsetto had vanished, replaced by a rich, feminine voice. My mouth dried instantly.

Even though I had become a believer in the arcane and the unexplainable, panic still tightened somewhere deep inside me. Fight or flight rebirthed the cynic. I silently rebuked myself, convincing myself it was probably nothing more than a clever parlour trick; one carefully tailored to impress the easily persuaded.

An old mentalist's trick.

I knew you were coming before you came through the door.

'I've been waiting for you the whole night! What took you so long?'

Caught completely off guard by her directness, I began explaining that I hadn't known about the street, or the little shop tucked away at its end, until that very night.

She cut me off.

Without another word she turned, beckoning me through the low doorway and into the dimly lit sanctum of her consultation room.

The room was filled with what an untrained eye might have dismissed as rubbish.

Bookshelves sagged beneath musty volumes. Dust-covered jars held preserved beasties and unidentifiable body parts. African and Japanese masks mingled with strange magical paraphernalia gathered from far-flung places. Some looked frightening, others lewd, all of them coated in a fine layer of dust.

Charts, diagrams and faded pictures covered the walls. Everything appeared to have been arranged to draw the eye towards a single point just off the centre of the room.

There stood a sturdy Ottoman draped in richly patterned cloth, probably printed somewhere in Asia from the look of it, blocking a narrow, book-lined passage leading to the staircase beyond.

Beside it sat a large leather armchair that seemed to dominate the room.

Madame Bea produced a ridiculously long pipe, lit it, then settled heavily into the leather chair, puffing on it with obvious satisfaction. With her free hand she patted the Ottoman beside her, inviting me to take a seat. I hesitated. As I did, the cat came running out of the shadows and leapt onto the Ottoman before I could sit down. It hissed at me in the most unwelcome manner.

'Ha, ha!' laughed Madame Bea. 'Looks like my cat doesn't like you. Edward doesn't usually take too warmly to strangers, do you now, Eddie?'

I didn't think the cat liked me very much either. I

hesitated once more. Then, in a swift movement, I reached forward and carefully picked him up. Edward spat at me and sank his claws into my hand. Placing him gently on the floor, I quickly sat down before he decided to reclaim my seat.

It was then that she said it. She leaned towards me and, in a strange, hollow voice, told me that I had loved someone too much in my previous life… and that I still loved her. That, she said, was my problem.

It felt as though I had been falling backwards onto the Ottoman for a very long time. Her words echoed through my mind. When my back finally met the worn fabric, my hands instinctively folded across my stomach.

As I lay there, I realised what I truly wanted from Madame Bea wasn't some startling revelation about my life. I already knew most things about myself.

What I desperately needed was someone to talk to.

Someone who would understand.

Someone who believed me.

So I lay back on the worn Ottoman and listened while she puffed quietly on her pipe. Seeds crackled and popped inside the bowl. Then I spoke.

'I can remember it all. In detail. Every wrinkle. Every minute.'

She sat just beyond the edge of my vision. I could barely

make out her wrinkled hand wrapped around the stem of the pipe, hear the soft smack of her lips as she drew deeply from it. Aromatic smoke curled lazily over my head, drifting upwards before gathering into monstrous shapes upon the walls.

She said nothing. So I continued.

'I remember every moment of my past life as though it happened yesterday. I remember whom I loved, and her memory haunts me. Every minute, every hour, is filled with thoughts of her.'

My eyes welled as I spoke.

'I remember the sound of her voice... the scent of her skin... and how the line of her neck curved into the soft space beneath her chin. I remember how she smiled. Her laughter. The way she cried.'

Madame Bea snapped her fingers three times.

I stopped, waiting for something to happen.

Nothing did. So I carried on.

'I can't get her out of my head or my heart. I know she's out there somewhere. I feel as though I have to find her in this life... or I'll go insane. I'll lose my mind.'

'Abe... have you consulted a psychotherapist?'

The question caught me completely off guard.

'You don't believe me?'

Silence settled over the room.

Finally she spoke.

'I believe you. But perhaps a doctor could give you something to help you forget. To dull the pain. It's a possible solution.'

'I don't want to forget. I want to feel. Feeling means I won't forget her, and not forgetting is what keeps me searching.'

'Do you think she's looking for you?'

I didn't know what to say.

Eventually I answered.

'I don't know.

'I hope so.'

'Why?'

'Because I have memories of her.'

'But those are your memories. She may not remember the same things.'

'We all remember on some level, don't we? Holding another person's hand... in a time before this one. Can we ever truly forget?'

Madame Bea drew slowly on her pipe. The quiet sound of her lips against the stem was the only noise in the room.

'Some remember more than others,' I continued. 'I think children remember best of all.'

'Some only wish to forget and never remember at all.'

She interrupted me.

'So... you came here to ask me something?'

I was beginning to think Madame Bea might be a cynic.

'I don't really have any questions...'

I stopped.

Then they all arrived at once.

'Well... perhaps I do. I wondered whether you could find out... I mean ask... whether she's alive in this life. Whether she lives in Memphis.'

I tried to sit up.

Madame Bea placed a firm hand on my shoulder and gently pushed me back.

'Is there any way of finding out?'

'I can ask.'

She paused.

'Whether we receive an answer is another matter.'

'Okay.'

She picked up a pack of tarot cards.

From the pack she drew a single card.

It shimmered in the dim light, vibrating almost imperceptibly, as though it possessed a life of its own. I watched as she laid it carefully upon the low table between us.

The card moved.

It glowed.

Jupiter.

Madame Bea's expression never changed.

'First... tell me more about your memories.'

'There's one memory I wake to every morning. Like clockwork. Always at exactly the same place. The same moment. It's the memory that drives me... perhaps the reason I've spent so long trying to find her.'

'Yes?'

Madame Bea reignited her pipe.

The flare from the lighter briefly illuminated the bridge of her nose before disappearing into darkness.

'Start with that one.'

I lay back and swallowed.

My memories swept over me.

Images and sensations turned like pages in the wind. As I travelled backwards through them, I reached a point where it felt as though I had stepped through a doorway.

Everything became beautifully clear.

My mouth continued speaking, describing every detail.

But I was no longer lying on the Ottoman.

I was inside the memory once again.

Watching it unfold.

Exactly as I had so many times before.

'I made a promise...'

My voice sounded impossibly far away.

The Lovers

Chapter two

Os amantes

The Lovers

We were young adventurers, determined to leave behind the rustic life of the countryside for the allure of the city. Every whispered plan, every secret coin saved, felt like a tiny rebellion against the world that had tried to cage us. Together, we slipped away from the disapproval of our parents, from the narrow routines and cautious watchfulness of the town that had always felt too tight for the life we imagined. The morning we left, the streets seemed impossibly long, stretching towards a horizon full of promise, and the air carried a taste of freedom we had never known.

Fortune smiled upon us. We found a modest, cosy council house tucked away in a quiet, unassuming city neighbourhood, a place that felt like it had been waiting for us all along. The houses were packed close together, neat rows of brick with narrow strips of grass separating them, each with a back garden long enough to escape into but just narrow enough to feel intimate. The streets were hushed in the early evening, the occasional distant laugh or barking dog echoing faintly, giving the area a quiet vitality that suited us perfectly. Every corner we turned felt familiar almost immediately, every pathway a tiny discovery, and in that tucked-away enclave we found a home of our own. The neighbourhood became our own little world, private and safe, yet brimming with possibility.

After a day of hard work, I would cycle home, passing those pristine, powdery pastel façades—narrow, muted headstones arranged in an endless line. If she hadn't been waiting for me at the end of that soul-crushing ride, I might have torn my own eyes out in despair. But I knew she would be there. Always, without fail, laughing as I clumsily pedalled up to our front path. I believed I would always be there for her too. Our relationship wasn't one of master and servant; we were equals, bound by a love that let us meet each other's gaze without flinching. Yet I couldn't shake the feeling that my love depended on hers, and I feared that made me selfish.

As I sat on my bicycle, suspended within the realm of my living memory, the sky darkened. A voice echoed from a break in the clouds, softly saying, 'Stop.' It was Madame Bea, entering my private world. At that moment, halfway down the street, I halted. 'Look around you,' the voice instructed. 'Try to understand where you are. Is there anything that can help you?' I inhaled deeply, realising I was in a lucid dream. My breath plumed out in front of me as I turned my head. In the distance, down a nearby road, I spotted something familiar—unmistakable architecture I knew well: the Art Deco façade of The Standard.

'Do you see it?' the voice asked.

I nodded.

'Okay, move on now.'

I got back on my bike and continued down the road. I understood then that we were in the city of Memphis. That my previous life had been in the same city I now lived in.

On our days off, we would stroll hand in hand to the park, just down the road from our little house. It was vast, with rolling lawns of neatly trimmed grass. Flowers of every kind filled the well-maintained beds, and grand old trees cast deep, soothing shade over cheerful groves. The turbulence of the recent war had subsided somewhat, and an uneasy peace had settled in. I cherished those walks. Sometimes, we packed a picnic basket and swung it between us as we walked, filled with happiness. We would spread our blanket on the gentle slope of a hill, overlooking the landscape stretching out like a dream below us. Beyond the jagged treetops, rows of houses with red roofs marked the park's outer edge, a tamed piece of nature within the expanding urban landscape.

On that day, the day of this specific memory, she was wearing a beautiful blue dress. I loved that dress, the way it draped her gentle frame. Her light brown eyes, kissed by heaven with flecks of green, sparkled in the late afternoon sun. I drowned a million times in those eyes. Every time I looked at her, pulled into her magnetic orbit, I found myself utterly lost. I don't think she ever fully grasped the effect she had on me. When I told her how she made me feel, she'd say I did the same to her. We were young and hopelessly in love.

Marrying your childhood sweetheart is a rare kind of intimacy, the sort where lives fold together so seamlessly that memory itself feels shared. Our histories intertwined before we even fully understood them—small moments magnified, ordinary streets and back gardens becoming stages for a private kind of magic. From the very first day we met on that narrow pavement, drawn to each other across the sun-baked tarmac like magnets, I knew our connection was singular. The road that divided her side of the street from mine felt suddenly irrelevant, just a thin line in a much larger orbit that was pulling us together.

I remember that first encounter as if the world had slowed to watch us—the way she hung upside down from the ancient tree in her garden, sunlight flickering through her hair, every movement effortless and alive. My words tumbled out in a mix of awe and hesitation, and for a heartbeat I wondered if she would topple too. But she didn't. She called down to me with that unshakable confidence that had always drawn me in, and in that moment everything about fear and caution melted away. Climbing after her was reckless, foolish, and yet necessary, as if the act itself cemented the invisible bond forming between us. High above the red soil, perched in the forked tangle of trunk and branches,

I realised a world I hadn't known existed—one where she and I could be untethered from all that constrained us. The tree swayed beneath us, almost breathing, almost alive. Our first kiss came much later—small, fleeting, but monumental in the memory of my young heart—a promise written in those moments of shared vertigo, a spark igniting a fire that would never fade.

Even as life around us bristled with opposition—familial rules, whispered admonitions, the wary glances of those who couldn't understand the gravity of our connection—we continued. Every day together was a quiet rebellion, a testament to the depth of the bond we had discovered. We became attuned to each other in ways that defied explanation, anticipating thoughts, sharing desires, and laughing in perfect synchrony at the absurdity of the world outside our orbit. No obstacle seemed large enough to keep us apart; distance, disapproval, and the weight of growing up could not diminish the flame that had ignited in our hearts so early.

When the time came to step fully into adulthood, we did so without hesitation, leaving behind the narrow streets and small houses that had first borne witness to our connection. We married quietly, legally, in a small government office, sealing our bond in a world that might not yet have been ready for it. Our lives together in that tiny house felt intensely private, fiercely our own. Work and daily routines came and went, but always we returned to one another, drawn by gravity, by the unspoken promise of belonging. Perhaps it was that very intensity, the luminous devotion that radiated between us, that had unsettled those who tried to contain us. Few could understand a flame burning so clearly and completely—only those who carried it themselves could know its warmth.

My mind returned to that afternoon in the park and her blue dress. In my memory, we sat on our usual peaceful slope, overlooking the tranquil park below. I had brought home a bottle of fine red wine, hidden in a brown paper bag, with the playful intention of sharing it there. We were celebrating—a month in our new house, a month of our new life together. Tucked away in my jacket pocket was a bar of her favourite chocolate, a special treat given our modest earnings at the time. I managed to surprise her, and I loved watching the genuine delight spread across her face. We kissed beneath the dappled shade of the trees, lying on our blanket beneath our leafy sanctuary. As we kissed, she suddenly pulled back to look into my eyes, her happiness clouded by a darker thought.

'I have this terrible premonition,' she said, her voice trembling. 'A storm is coming.'

Her eyes, once bright, turned a dull grey.

I laughed, glancing up at the clear, peaceful sky above us, but a sudden gust of wind tousled her hair and sent a chill through my heart.

'Not today. The sky is beautifully blue and clear,' I said,

trying to reassure her.

She looked at me sadly, a gentle smile tugging at the corners of her mouth.

'It's as if invisible dark clouds are passing over me… over my mind.'

She nervously bit the skin around her fingertips, her eyes gleaming as though hiding some inner light. I was completely mystified by her.

'I saw something terrible on my way home today,' she whispered, her voice barely audible above the rustling leaves.

I tried to lighten the mood with a silly joke, but she wouldn't have it.

'It was awful. A man collapsed in the queue ahead of me. He just crumpled to the ground with barely a sound. His arms and legs shook uncontrollably. I wanted to help, but I didn't know what to do. There were people between us. His eyes rolled back, and he thrashed about like a fish out of water. I can't get him out of my mind. Every time I close my eyes, I see him struggling, like a fish desperate to find its way back to the ocean.'

Tears welled in her eyes, and I could see the storm she had spoken of brewing inside her. She was lost in her own memory, unreachable for a moment. I dared not speak.

'Then his wife arrived. She stood to one side, her hands

covering her mouth, sobbing, crying, screaming for help. I wanted to run and hide, like I did as a child, but I just stood there, watching in horrified fascination. He was gurgling and choking, struggling to breathe. The smell… it was terrible, just terrible. And then he stopped moving. Suddenly, everything was still. The people in the shop, those who had seen it all happen, stared blankly at each other, then at the man on the floor. I could see the guilt in their eyes—guilt for feeling relieved that it was over, that the horror had ended. The shop assistant had called the hospital, but it was too late. You could have heard a whisper from miles away in that silence. His eyes glazed over, and he was gone. His body seemed to deflate, sinking into the ground like a balloon losing air. His poor wife dropped her purse. It felt like an eternity before it finally hit the floor. She kept repeating his name, over and over. I remember thinking that his name sounded familiar, like yours or my brother's. They had been together for thirty years. Tomorrow would have been their thirty-first anniversary.'

I watched her closely as she recounted the awful events of that day. I could sense this moment mattered, that it was shaping something deep within her. She looked into my eyes, and for a moment it felt as though the whole world existed only within her gaze.

'What happens when we die?' she asked, tears gathering once more in the corners of her eyes. 'Will I ever see you again? Or do we just fade into silent darkness, cease to exist, with everything we once were simply gone?'

I frowned, unsure of what to say.

'What would you like to happen?' I asked, my voice faltering.

'I want us to live forever,' she replied instantly, without hesitation or doubt.

'Well... I don't think that's possible.'

We both knew it wasn't, but my words still made her face fall. She needed something more from me, and I had let her down.

Desperate to comfort her, I tried again.

'Remember Wallace Hammond?'

She nodded, brushing her tear-streaked hair away from her face.

'He left after sixth form and joined some group that meditates in the woods for days, saying he could feel the energy of the trees. Anyway, I ran into him at the corner shop about four months ago. We went to the same school, but I hardly recognised him. He was wearing this long smock, with a long beard and hair. The shop owner kept calling him Jesus as a joke. We got to talking, and he seemed convinced that when we die, we don't just disappear. He believed we come back, living life over and over again.'

I smiled gently and held her hand.

'What if that's true? What if, after we die, we come back in another form, as different people... for whatever reason?'

Her eyes widened, and I could almost feel her heart racing. I had never seen her so vulnerable. She had always been the stronger, more certain one between us.

'Promise me you'll find me in the next life,' she said, her voice filled with an intensity that swept over me like a wave of fire. 'No matter what happens, say you'll find me.'

It was a leap of faith into the unknown.

'I... will...' I stuttered. 'I promise I'll find you. You know I'll love you forever.'

And I did. I loved her passionately, without reservation.

'Marry me again in the next life?' she asked, smiling as she curled into me.

'In this and every lifetime,' I replied, holding her close as we sipped wine from the bottle and nibbled on chocolate.

She accepted it as the truth, as though it were the most natural explanation of life's mysteries. But for me, it was a comforting story to ease her fears, not something I fully believed. Her desperation left a hole inside me, a gnawing fear that one day death would take her away, and there would be nothing I could do to stop it.

We lay there, watching people enjoy the park, with kites

soaring high above us. I could sense she was still deep in thought, her body shifting restlessly as she nestled into my chest.

'How will we know?' she asked abruptly.

'Huh?' I replied, caught off guard.

'How will I know it's you? How will you know it's me?' She looked up at me, her eyes searching for answers, as though trying to unravel a logic that could make everything clear.

I chuckled at her seriousness, which only made her sit up, frowning at my lack of concern.

'We'll just know,' I said with a shrug. 'There'll be something that makes it obvious.'

'A sign?'

I nodded.

She relaxed back against my chest.

That was the end of it. We never spoke about it again, lying there on our blanket in our little paradise, with dozens of kites painting the sky in vibrant colours. We laughed, cracked jokes, sipped red wine, and savoured the last of our dark chocolate. As the afternoon wore on, the chocolate was gone, and she began tying the wrapper into a little knot—an automatic habit that always fascinated me. It was one of the ways I always knew she'd been sneaking sweets. I'd find those wrappers tied into loopy ribbons scattered around the house. I picked one up and smiled at her.

'You've turned this into an art form.'

She answered with nothing but a radiant smile and a playful, guilty giggle.

We packed up our things not long afterwards, stumbling back through the park, the winding path leading us home to our narrow street lined with neat little houses. By the time we reached our door, strange grey clouds had gathered overhead, and a cold wind whipped down the pavement, sending dead leaves swirling in violent gusts. As I stood at the front door, I glanced back at the dark shadows pooling beneath the trees and in the corners of the street. They seemed to move, as though they were coming for us.

And they did.

Madame Bea interrupted again, this time with three sharp claps of her hands. Crisp. Insistent. The sound jolted me from my trance, reverberating through the quiet room like a warning. She paused, one hand suspended in the air, and for a moment I thought she had noticed something... something that wasn't right. Her eyes narrowed slightly, a flicker of tension crossing her normally composed features before she drew in a slow, deliberate breath.

Then, almost as if regaining control of herself, she returned to the array of tarot cards spread meticulously across the ornate wooden table beside the Ottoman.

Yet something had changed. Her movements were smaller now, more deliberate. Every shuffle and placement felt measured, as though she were testing the edges of some hidden truth. She puffed furiously on her pipe, the smoke curling through the dim light, and for the first time those twisting tendrils seemed to cling to the air with an almost unnatural weight.

Jupiter still shone and vibrated faintly beside me, but even that familiar presence seemed subdued, as if it too sensed the undercurrent of unease threading through the room. Madame Bea's fingers hovered above the cards, lingering over one in particular before allowing it to slide into place. Her eyes, once steady and sure, flicked briefly towards the shadows gathering in the corners of the room, and for a heartbeat I understood that whatever the cards were revealing had unsettled her.

'So... that's her?' she asked, the flare from her pipe casting an almost unnatural glow across her face as she inhaled deeply.

Her words sliced through the silence, dragging me abruptly from my reverie. The room suddenly felt smaller, the air tighter, as though the walls themselves had leaned in to listen. She held my gaze, yet somehow seemed to be looking beyond me, reading a truth I could not yet comprehend.

'Yes,' I mumbled, my throat tightening, my hands

curling inward as though trying to restrain the tide of emotion rising inside me. 'That's her. That's why I'm searching for her. I promised I would—even when I didn't believe it myself. I loved her, and I said I'd find her no matter what. I still love her. It's not something I can control. Believe me... I tried.'

My voice cracked, the words spilling into the room like a tide I could no longer hold back, echoing softly from the walls before disappearing into the curling smoke.

Madame Bea said nothing. She didn't even glance up. Her attention remained fixed on the cards, though the rigidity of her posture betrayed an unease she could no longer conceal. Her hands hovered over the deck for longer than seemed necessary, fingers twitching as though searching for some hidden fault line. She shifted one card, then another—deliberate, precise—as though navigating a labyrinth only she could perceive.

Then, almost violently, another card emerged from

the pack.

The Sun.

It blazed in her hands, a sudden flare of warmth and light that seemed almost alive, and she placed it carefully beside Jupiter. The cards hummed in response, a subtle vibration that tightened my stomach and sent a shiver racing up my spine. Their glow caught in her eyes, revealing something I had never seen before.

Fear.

'Unnatural,' she said, her voice low and dry, yet sharp enough to make me flinch. 'You shouldn't remember any of that. It's better to let those memories go. That life is gone. Focus on living this one.'

Although she spoke calmly, agitation rippled beneath every word, as though my memories had disturbed something far greater than either of us understood. The unease in her eyes settled over me, cold and undeniable, coiling around my chest like a living thing.

'No!' I shouted. 'I won't lose her again!'

Her expression softened, maternal yet firm, as she regarded me like a child in need of guidance.

'You had a lifetime with her,' she said. 'You can't have another. If it were meant to be, you would have found her by now… or you will, in time. Stop searching.'

'I lost her!' I cried. 'Don't you understand? Within a month, everything was gone!'

I tried to rise from the Ottoman, but she held me down with a strength that was both overpowering and unnerving. Trembling, I sank back onto the cushion.

'Not yet,' she warned.

She rose and crossed to an emerald jar etched with intricate symbols. Dipping her hand inside, she retrieved a moist, sticky substance and carefully refilled her pipe. With a flourish, she lit it once more, the hazy smoke curling around me, softening the edge of my panic, coaxing me towards a fragile calm.

'Tell me more,' she said, exhaling slowly. 'Then what?'

We lay there, watching people enjoy the park, with kites soaring high above us. I could sense she was still deep in thought, her body shifting restlessly as she nestled into my chest.

‘How will we know?’ she asked abruptly.

‘Huh?’ I replied, caught off guard.

‘How will I know it’s you? How will you know it’s me?’ She looked up at me, her eyes searching for answers, as though trying to unravel a logic that could make everything clear.

I chuckled at her seriousness, which only made her sit up, frowning at my lack of concern.

‘We’ll just know,’ I said with a shrug. ‘There’ll be something that makes it obvious.’

‘A sign?’

I nodded.

She relaxed back against my chest.

That was the end of it. We never spoke about it again, lying there on our blanket in our little paradise, with dozens of kites painting the sky in vibrant colours. We laughed, cracked jokes, sipped red wine, and savoured the last of our dark chocolate. As the afternoon wore on, the chocolate was gone, and she began tying the wrapper into a little knot—an automatic habit that always fascinated me. It was one of the ways I always knew she’d been sneaking sweets. I’d find those wrappers tied into loopy ribbons scattered around the house. I picked one up and smiled at her.

‘You’ve turned this into an art form.’

She answered with nothing but a radiant smile and a

playful, guilty giggle.

We packed up our things not long afterwards, stumbling back through the park, the winding path leading us home to our narrow street lined with neat little houses. By the time we reached our door, strange grey clouds had gathered overhead, and a cold wind whipped down the pavement, sending dead leaves swirling in violent gusts. As I stood at the front door, I glanced back at the dark shadows pooling beneath the trees and in the corners of the street. They seemed to move, as though they were coming for us.

And they did.

Madame Bea interrupted again, this time with three sharp claps of her hands. Crisp. Insistent. The sound jolted me from my trance, reverberating through the quiet room like a warning. She paused, one hand suspended in the air, and for a moment I thought she had noticed something... something that wasn't right. Her eyes narrowed slightly, a flicker of tension crossing her normally composed features before she drew in a slow, deliberate breath.

Then, almost as if regaining control of herself, she returned to the array of tarot cards spread meticulously across the ornate wooden table beside the Ottoman. Yet something had changed. Her movements were smaller now, more deliberate. Every shuffle and placement felt measured, as though she were testing the edges of some hidden truth. She puffed furiously on her pipe, the smoke curling through the dim light, and for the first time those twisting tendrils seemed to cling to the air with an almost unnatural weight.

Jupiter still shone and vibrated faintly beside me, but even that familiar presence seemed subdued, as if it too sensed the undercurrent of unease threading through the room. Madame Bea's fingers hovered above the cards, lingering over one in particular before allowing it to slide into place. Her eyes, once steady and sure, flicked briefly towards the shadows gathering in the corners of the room, and for a heartbeat I understood that whatever the cards were revealing had unsettled her.

'So... that's her?' she asked, the flare from her pipe casting an almost unnatural glow across her face as she inhaled deeply.

Her words sliced through the silence, dragging me abruptly from my reverie. The room suddenly felt smaller, the air tighter, as though the walls themselves had leaned in to listen. She held my gaze, yet somehow seemed to be looking beyond me, reading a truth I could not yet comprehend.

'Yes,' I mumbled, my throat tightening, my hands curling inward as though trying to restrain the tide of emotion rising inside me. 'That's her. That's why I'm searching for her. I promised I would—even when I didn't believe it myself. I loved her, and I said I'd find her no matter what. I still love her. It's not something I can control. Believe me... I tried.'

My voice cracked, the words spilling into the room like a tide I could no longer hold back, echoing softly from the walls before disappearing into the curling smoke.

Madame Bea said nothing. She didn't even glance up. Her attention remained fixed on the cards, though the rigidity of her posture betrayed an unease she could no longer conceal. Her hands hovered over the deck for longer than seemed necessary, fingers twitching as though searching for some hidden fault line. She shifted one card, then another—deliberate, precise—as though navigating a labyrinth only she could perceive.

Then, almost violently, another card emerged from the pack.

The Sun.

It blazed in her hands, a sudden flare of warmth and light that seemed almost alive, and she placed it carefully beside Jupiter. The cards hummed in response, a subtle vibration that tightened my stomach and sent a shiver racing up my spine. Their glow caught in her eyes, revealing something I had never seen before.

Fear.

'Unnatural,' she said, her voice low and dry, yet sharp enough to make me flinch. 'You shouldn't remember any of that. It's better to let those memories go. That life is gone. Focus on living this one.'

Although she spoke calmly, agitation rippled beneath

every word, as though my memories had disturbed something far greater than either of us understood. The unease in her eyes settled over me, cold and undeniable, coiling around my chest like a living thing.

'No!' I shouted. 'I won't lose her again!'

Her expression softened, maternal yet firm, as she regarded me like a child in need of guidance.

'You had a lifetime with her,' she said. 'You can't have another. If it were meant to be, you would have found her by now... or you will, in time. Stop searching.'

'I lost her!' I cried. 'Don't you understand? Within a month, everything was gone!'

I tried to rise from the Ottoman, but she held me down with a strength that was both overpowering and unnerving. Trembling, I sank back onto the cushion.

'Not yet,' she warned.

She rose and crossed to an emerald jar etched with intricate symbols. Dipping her hand inside, she retrieved a moist, sticky substance and carefully refilled her pipe. With a flourish, she lit it once more, the hazy smoke curling around me, softening the edge of my panic, coaxing me towards a fragile calm.

'Tell me more,' she said, exhaling slowly. 'Then what?'

Death

Chapter three

Morte

Death

I felt myself slipping back into a haze, drawn into a different dimension, the separate reality of my memory. As I descended into it, a thought flickered through my mind: *Are our minds doorways to these alternate realms?* But there was no time to ponder, as the familiar clarity of the past enveloped me, drawing me into a scene that unfolded before my eyes.

Less than a week after our conversation in the park, chaos erupted. The fiery red horseman of the apocalypse had descended upon the world, dragging us into its destructive wake. War had broken out again, and we were caught in its merciless grip. Like countless other young men, I received my conscription papers. The turmoil swept us towards transport hubs, carrying us to the expanding conflict. Soon, I found myself at the central train station, crammed onto an outbound platform with my sobbing young wife in my arms.

We weren't alone.

The air was thick with anxiety as thousands of us passed through the station each week, destined for makeshift camps and the front lines.

The camps we were sent to were hardly camps at all—more like holding pens scattered along the edge of the front, so close we could almost taste the gun smoke drifting on the wind. We were little more than boys, herded from stations to tents, watching trains vanish into the haze as others arrived to take their place. Our desperate leaders had neglected to give us any prior training before thrusting us into those camps. We were told we'd receive the only instruction we needed: how to hold a rifle and charge headlong into a storm of bullets fired by faceless enemies. No drills. No discipline. Just a grim faith that instinct and fear would do the rest. It was clear, even then, that none of us was ready.

Steam and smoke from the engines choked the air. In the dim light, I stared at my train, dazed. My wife clung to me, her despair reflected in the faces of the other young men around us, gathered like cattle waiting to be led to slaughter.

'Don't go,' she gasped, her voice trembling. 'We can escape. I have family far away who will take us in. We can hide.'

Her arms tightened around me, and I couldn't bear it. The previous night had been a torment of waiting, each minute dragging us closer to my departure.

'You know that won't work,' I murmured, resting my face against her shoulder, feeling the warmth of her skin. 'I love you. You know I don't want to go.'

Our eyes met for a brief, agonising moment.

'But I have no choice.'

She refused to let go, her tears soaking into my coat. Whistles blared in the distance, and shouts echoed through the station, urging the young men to board. Uniformed officers carrying clubs began forcing us away from our loved ones and towards the open carriages.

I looked into her eyes, overwhelmed by grief and the cruelty of our fate.

'I won't let you go! I'm coming with you!' she screamed.

Military police came barrelling towards us.

I lifted her into my arms and kissed her one final time, defiantly, before one of the officers wrenched me away. She lunged at the men dragging me, shouting, 'Don't die! Come back to me!'

They pulled me into a cramped compartment already filled with other despondent men.

The carriage was packed and stifling. I fought my way back to a grimy, steamed-up window and pressed myself against it. Wedging my fingers into the narrow gap, I managed to slide the pane down a few inches.

I called her name.

Amid the confusion outside, I finally saw her.

She was running towards the window, reaching out to me. Blood was smeared across her cheek from the struggle. A surge of anger and helplessness gripped me. Standing on tiptoes, she gazed up as I crushed myself against the opening, stretching my arm just far enough to touch her cheek.

'I love you,' I choked, tears threatening to overwhelm me.

'I'm going to lose you!' she sobbed. 'Don't go! I can feel it. I just know I'll lose you!'

She pounded the side of the train with her fists.

The train lurched into motion, beginning its slow departure. Metal screeched. Whistles pierced the air. Great clouds of steam billowed around us. The platform started to drift away, but she clung desperately to my hand until the train gathered speed and the end of the platform drew near.

Realising these might be our final moments together,

she ran alongside the train, desperate to keep my eyes locked on hers until the platform finally defeated her.

'Don't forget your promise,' she cried. 'Don't forget me.'

We both feared I would never return, that the war would claim me as it would millions of others.

I pressed my face against the narrow opening of the window, straining for one last glimpse of her. I watched until she disappeared into the distance, my vision blurring as I leaned against the unyielding glass.

When she finally vanished from sight, I was left with the unbearable certainty that I had seen her for the last time.

Madame Bea returned, her eyes fixed on me as she wistfully puffed on her curved pipe. The strange substance inside glowed softly, casting an otherworldly light across her face and drawing my attention back to the room.

'So... you died?' she asked, seeking clarity.

'Yes,' I replied, surfacing briefly from my memories before sinking into them once more, as though diving into a vast, dark ocean.

This time, I found myself on the front line, on the day I died.

The men around us had dug deep trenches filled with water, blood and sewage. We were dying from disease almost as quickly as from the relentless hail of bullets and shells. I had been there for less than a week, yet many of the men who had arrived with me were already dead or gravely wounded. The injured were carried away to grim, blood-soaked tents run by medics and bone surgeons. Survival often meant enduring horrific wounds and the ever-present threat of sepsis. If you survived both, you could finally go home—a twisted way of escaping the front forever.

Every day, new faces arrived, only to

vanish almost immediately, replaced by others in a relentless cycle. We all knew it was only a matter of time before our turn came. Eventually, our bodies would be discarded into some mass grave, just like those who had fallen before us.

I survived long enough to receive a letter from her, delicately scented with her favourite perfume. For a minute or two, the fragrance transformed the trench into a haven of warmth and hope. I never got to read the letter in full.

I was crouched beneath a makeshift wooden shelter, trying to escape the rain, when I was interrupted. Our sergeant was calling us, ordering us to climb over the battlements and out of the trench for another offensive. We were to push forward on the eastern front and reclaim lost ground.

I quickly tucked the letter into my breast pocket, grabbed my rifle, and followed my comrades up and out of the pit.

We huddled behind piles of rubble and mounds of earth just above the trenches, our rifles at the ready. We were a ragtag group of young men, barely adults, roughnecks and well-bred alike, united in our grim task. The command came down the line.

We charged.

Cannons roared. Bullets whined overhead. The cacophony of battle drove us forward as we crouched, then ran, firing our rifles into the smoke-filled void ahead.

When it happened, I felt no pain—only a dull pressure between my eyes, as though someone had

pressed hard against my skull. I lost control of my limbs and collapsed into the mud.

As my body struck the ground, I realised I was dead.

Yet I was no longer inside my body.

I found myself standing beside my lifeless form, observing the glassy eyes of my own corpse with detached curiosity.

Looking beyond it, I saw the battlefield strewn with other spectral figures of fallen men. Some were already wandering aimlessly away from their physical remains. A grim procession of the dead stretched behind us. Everywhere I looked, the fallen were rising as ghostly replicas of themselves. They appeared bewildered, uncertain. The sounds of battle had become strangely muted, as though the war already belonged to another world.

I tried to retrieve the letter from my pocket, but it remained stubbornly out of reach. Looking down at my hands and then at my ghostly form, I noticed my uniform was clean, untouched by blood or mud. Above me, the sky had become a grey haze, black smoke staining the distant horizon. I turned away from the battlefield and walked on, avoiding strange bursts of light that appeared without warning, gathering the spirits of the dead. Their presence felt frantic, almost desperate, and so I kept moving, putting as much distance between myself and them as I could.

I wandered farther from the front until I came upon a semi-transparent stairway rising into the fading sky.

Something within me knew I had to climb it.

I reached for the railing.

Yet a deep sense of unfinished business held me back, her presence lingering like a quiet reminder of something left undone. I should have gone back to her. I should have said goodbye.

But I was dead.

And I was lost.

I didn't know how to find her.

Sadness and regret settled heavily upon me as I climbed, pausing often as the staircase spiralled ever upwards. Around me, the sky was wrapped in profound silence. I wondered why I had chosen silence over her. I wondered whether I had ever truly been given a choice.

The answer never came.

Sometimes the silence became so complete that I felt myself flickering in and out of existence, like a faulty lightbulb glowing in the dark. Up there, the universe stretched endlessly around me, like an immense tablecloth unfurling in every direction, everything drifting with no clear sense of where I began or ended. Strange beings floated through the vastness, their voices echoing softly as they dispensed their poultices of light. Surrounded by an overwhelming sense of love, I drifted through the endless expanse, wrapped in the mystery of it all.

Gradually, the world began to solidify.

Ahead of me stretched a procession of figures, perhaps the dead, clothed in robes with veils covering their faces. They moved slowly along an ornate passage before crossing a bridge towards a towering wall with a single entrance set into it.

At the foot of the wall stood a small door.

The figures were arranged in three rows. The middle row held the dead, dressed in robes of green and blue, separated by delicate lines of red. The outer rows were filled with their guides—those entrusted with helping the dead cross into the next world.

Each person stopped beside a small wooden table.

The guides standing on either side gestured towards it.

The dead placed objects upon its surface before passing through the doorway.

The objects lingered for a brief moment before dissolving
into vapour.

Then the next soul stepped forward.

I found myself carried gently into the procession, moving with a quiet inevitability. My guides walked beside me, smiling with a kindness that felt both ancient and familiar, as though they could see every joy

and every sorrow I had
ever carried. Together,
we crossed the
bridge, its
graceful arch
suspended like
a silver

ribbon above the abyss, until we reached the doorway waiting at the far end.

At the table, they gestured with calm reverence, their open hands revealing its purpose.

It was called the Table of Apologies and Forgiveness.

It was not a place of judgement, but of release.

Here, every attachment, every regret, every memory of those I had loved and lost could be laid down and allowed to dissolve into the quiet air.

I reached into the pockets of my robe and felt the familiar shapes of the objects I had carried for decades. Each memento bore the imprint of a life once lived—fragments of childhood, small tokens of love, reminders of moments both tender and fleeting. Slowly, deliberately, I held each one in my hand, felt its texture, remembered its story, and placed it upon the table.

There was something deeply peaceful about the ritual.

A quiet cleansing in letting them go.

But when I came to my wedding band, my fingers closed tightly around it, hiding it within my palm.

The guides' eyes lingered on my hand, but I kept the ring concealed, unwilling to surrender this final tether to the life I had loved so deeply.

Keeping it hidden against my skin, I lifted my gaze, lowered my head in silent resolve, and stepped through the doorway.

The threshold hummed beneath my feet.

The air shimmered with the echoes of everything I had left behind...

and with the faint promise of everything that still lay ahead.

The High Pries

Chapter four

A suma sacerdotisa

The High Priestess

'Stop!' Madame Bea shouted, her hand clamping over my mouth. 'Don't say another word! It's forbidden for me to know. For anyone to know! Do you remember the rites of the passage?'

Her eyes widened in terror, casting eerie shadows across her face.

'I... I don't understand,' I stammered, seized by an inexplicable guilt. I recoiled, shaken by the sudden change in her demeanour.

'You do remember!' she spat, making a frantic gesture with her free hand. 'It's true, isn't it? You don't just recall your past life, but the sacred space between this life and the next, do you?'

She recoiled from me as though I were contaminated, her face a mask of shock and dread. Her cat hissed from the corner, adding to the chaos.

Then it was gone.

Her reaction left me deeply unsettled.

'Well... yes, I suppose I do remember, but...' I faltered, struggling to find the right words.

'But? No "buts"!' She shoved me towards the waiting room. 'You have to leave! Get out before they find you! It's a miracle they haven't come for you yet! Three years? I hope they're not already outside waiting for you!'

In a frenzy, she hurled her lit pipe to the floor, sending her tarot cards scattering across the room. Their symbols became a jumbled confusion in the commotion, except for two that immediately caught my eye.

Jupiter.

The Sun.

A third card lay face up nearby, an icy light emanating from its surface.

The Moon.

I understood none of it.

'Who knows what they'll do to me if they find you

here!' she whimpered.

'Wait!' I protested, planting my feet as she tried to force me out. 'Wait a moment! You can't just throw me out! What about finding her? Help me! Can't you help me?'

I sank to my knees.

'Please. At least tell me if she's alive. Does she live in this city?'

Madame Bea remained unrelenting. Her presence seemed to swell, almost doubling in size. With surprising strength, she hauled me towards the front door. I resisted, throwing myself onto the floor and wedging my body between the benches and walls in a desperate attempt to stay.

She glared at me for a long moment.

Then she slumped to the floor beside the door.

'If I tell you, will you leave?' she asked, her voice weary.

'Yes! Yes, I promise! I'll never come back. I swear!'

She studied me with quiet sorrow.

'Okay,' Madame Bea said, rising abruptly. 'Wait here.'

She disappeared into the next room, and I heard hurried movement beyond the wall. My arm throbbed, so I sat on the bench, rubbing it while I waited.

When she returned, her face was pale, almost colourless, yet she managed a tired smile.

'She's alive. She's about your age. And there's more

good news—she lives in Memphis too. It seems you were both drawn back here, so you may be in luck.'

Her faint smile lingered as she watched the joy spread across my face. I thanked her over and over, kissing her hand in heartfelt gratitude.

'There's one more thing,' she said.

A chill crept down my spine at the change in her voice.

'There's a chance you might actually find her.'

She hesitated, wrestling with something she clearly wished she didn't have to say.

Finally, she spoke.

'The chances are good.'

'Thank you!' I exclaimed, tears filling my eyes as I reached for the door.

I opened it slightly and peered into the darkness outside.

Madame Bea pulled me back by the shoulder, her eyes wide with fear.

'Be careful! They'll come for you! They find everyone whose memory drifts into the space between lives. They must protect the sacred places.'

She stared anxiously into the night, as though something dreadful waited just beyond the darkness.

'Who will come for me? What will they do?' I asked, stepping outside before turning back to her.

She pulled the door almost closed, leaving only a narrow

gap through which one frightened eye watched me.

'The Jackal,' she whispered. 'The warden of the dead and the living. The keeper of secrets.'

She swallowed.

'I don't know what they'll do, Abe. They may take you away... or erase your memory, returning you to a walking slumber. Just don't mention me to them.'

'I won't. Thank you.'

Her expression softened.

'Don't mention it. I'm sorry I can't help you more. If you want to find her, you'd better hurry. If they decide you're a threat, they'll strip away your memories, and everything you've worked for will be lost.'

I backed away in stunned silence as she closed the door with a decisive thud.

The neon lights flickered out.

In their fading afterglow, Madame Bea's house resembled a tomb.

The shadows around me stirred.

And they were closer than before.

The Magician

Chapter five

O mágico

The Magician

My head felt impossibly heavy, every thought dragging me deeper, dark circles beneath my eyes as though I'd spent the night drowning in booze. I stumbled out of the maze of alleyways, an urban labyrinth where I had learned too late that trouble had been stalking me all along, gripping me tighter than I had ever realised. That night, deep in the heart of downtown, had been my last desperate attempt to find her—the woman who haunted my every waking thought.

I was ready to give up.

Finding Madame Bea felt like a consolation prize—or worse, a cruel reminder that this search had always been in vain.

The streets were full of drifters, lost souls searching for something, anything. But unlike the hollow-eyed junkies shuffling beside me each night, I wasn't trying to fill my life with meaning through dark compulsions. Yet there I was, night after night, drawn into the city's underbelly, searching for my own escape, my own fix. After three lonely, hollow years, I stood at the edge of my personal abyss, finally realising that my addiction was far darker, far more consuming than any of theirs.

I finally reached my car, parked against a crumbling kerb a few blocks away. While I'd been with Madame Bea, the day had quietly arrived. Beyond the thick shadows of the city, the sky held that eerie half-light that lingers before dawn. What I miss most about nights in the city is the absence of stars. The sky becomes a flat orange-black, a hollow space framed by towering buildings, even in the hours before sunrise.

But there is something constant, whether in the city or the countryside.

Those few sacred minutes of profound stillness before the world wakes.

The sun has yet to rise and won't for a while, but the air already hums with the promise of what is to come.

That night, under Madame Bea's guidance, I had

learned so much. I discovered that we had once lived in this very part of the city, now nothing more than its derelict inner core. I realised that The Standard had stood within sight of our old neighbourhood.

Exhaustion washed over me.

I slumped against the car door, resting my forehead on the cool glass of the driver's window. Tears slid down the bridge of my nose, splashing softly against the glass, the weight of three years of searching finally catching up with me. Yet despite everything Madame Bea had revealed, I still felt no closer to finding her.

As I turned my head, something flickered at the edge of my vision.

Between two crumbling warehouses, squeezed into the narrow gap between them, stood a relic from another age.

An old red-brick house with a weathered timber façade, faded to a lifeless grey and twisted by time.

It was exactly the sort of house I had described to Madame Bea barely an hour earlier.

It could have been any house from our old street.

Yet something about it stirred a forgotten echo of happiness buried deep inside me.

The sight jolted me awake.

I abandoned my plan to collapse onto my sofa and instead found myself drawn towards the house, as though it held answers I wasn't yet ready to face. I had parked on this street countless times.

How had I never noticed it before?

Standing at the edge of the property, I breathed slowly, deliberately, each breath steadying me as I studied the warped grey timbers. The blackened windows stared back, empty and accusing, while the boarded door seemed almost to mock me—taunting my failure to return home, to make peace with the past.

What happened when she received the news?

When did she learn I had been killed?

How did she live afterwards?

Did she remarry?

Did she forget me?

Had these three years of searching really been about redemption—an obsessive need to prove that she had loved me... or that I still loved her?

Or was it something darker?

Was she simply a ghost I refused to release?

A possession I couldn't bear to lose?

Standing before the ruined house beneath the violet light of dawn, I felt utterly broken. I could almost see her stepping onto our front path, looking for me as I cycled home up the hill.

Only...

I never came home.

What became of her after I died?

What kind of life did she live?

I hesitated at the foot of the porch, staring at the charred remains of the doorway. My stomach tightened, caught between the urge to step inside and the dread of what waited beyond it.

In the end, I turned away.

I could never return to what had once been our home.

Not without her.

Going back alone would have felt hollow, like ending my journey with a lie. I feared that crossing that threshold would unravel something inside me, destroying everything I had fought so hard to preserve.

My journey couldn't end here.

It could only end when I found her.

But would I finally feel whole when I did?

Perched on a low wall a few feet away sat what looked like a black cat.

Like a human.

Its legs dangled over the edge, its tail curled neatly beside it. Its belly was round and hairless, and beneath it hung two swollen, pink, hairless testicles. Disturbingly, there appeared to be no penis at all. Two short, goat-like horns protruded from its head.

The creature stared back at me with a tired, knowing expression, as though it had been waiting for me to judge it.

I stepped closer, my heart quickening.

'Edward?' I asked cautiously.

'Took you long enough,' the cat replied, sounding thoroughly unimpressed.

'What the hell is this? What are you doing here? And what are you? You're not a real cat, are you?'

'I'm a familiar spirit. Bea's familiar, to be exact. She asked me to keep an eye on you. Help if I can. So here I am.' Eddie shrugged. 'Not that I wanted the job.'

He hopped down from the wall, landing lightly before strolling away upright, his tail swaying behind him. Shaking a furry fist in my direction, he called back,

'Remember the bigger picture, Abe! Everything's connected.'

He didn't even look back.

'Right, I'm done. I'll come back if you start screwing things up—or if you forget your little promise not to blab to the enforcers. Got it?'

And then he was gone.

The first sliver of sunlight crept above the jagged eastern skyline, its pale light stinging my eyes, though its warmth was welcome against my cold skin. It had been a long, surreal night.

Then it struck me.

The cat hadn't been leading me to the house.

He had been leading me to a memory.

Finding the house had unlocked something deeper—a way to navigate the forgotten neighbourhood that had once surrounded it. I could now retrace the route we had walked so many years before.

Straight to the park.

That conversation in the park had changed everything.

It made perfect sense to begin there.

With renewed purpose, I set off down the street.

Our little neighbourhood, now consumed by anonymous warehouses, was almost unrecognisable after more than eighty years. Cracked pavements split beneath yellowed weeds, the broken concrete resembling an abstract painting conceived by a meth addict. I followed those fractured slabs—my own yellow brick road—around the corner.

At the end of the short street stood a small cluster of trees surrounding a frost-bitten patch of grass.

The last surviving fragment of our park.

It stood defiantly amidst the encroaching sea of brick and concrete.

Only a tiny remnant remained.

Yet I recognised it instantly.

Rubbing my face in disbelief, I walked towards a leaf-covered bench beneath a tall tree. Although it faced away from where we had once sat, I lowered myself onto it anyway, soaking in the first hesitant rays of morning sunlight.

The air was still bitterly cold. Darkness lingered in the narrow alleys and beneath the surrounding buildings.

Unlike the warehouses behind me, this neighbourhood still felt alive.

Five-storey flats and tightly packed terraced houses bordered the park. Independent businesses lined the street—a clothing shop, a children's day nursery, a delicatessen, a convenience store and other small shops that served the local community.

I shifted on the narrow wooden bench, trying to make myself comfortable.

Birds chirped overhead, late migrants not yet driven south by the coming winter.

Autumn was almost over.

Winter waited impatiently.

I was cold.

And utterly exhausted.

Then, suddenly, warm lights flared to life in the building across the street.

I had planned to sit quietly in the park and reconnect with the place that had once held so much of our happiness, but fatigue clung to me, deep in my bones. Across the road, the lights glowed invitingly behind softly decorated windows.

My tired mind finally focused on the words painted above the door.

It was a café.

The rich aroma of fresh coffee drifted towards me.

I slowly climbed to my feet and crossed the empty road.

A small sign hung in the centre of the glass door.

Come in and let go of your sorrows.

The Star

Chapter six

A estrela

The Star

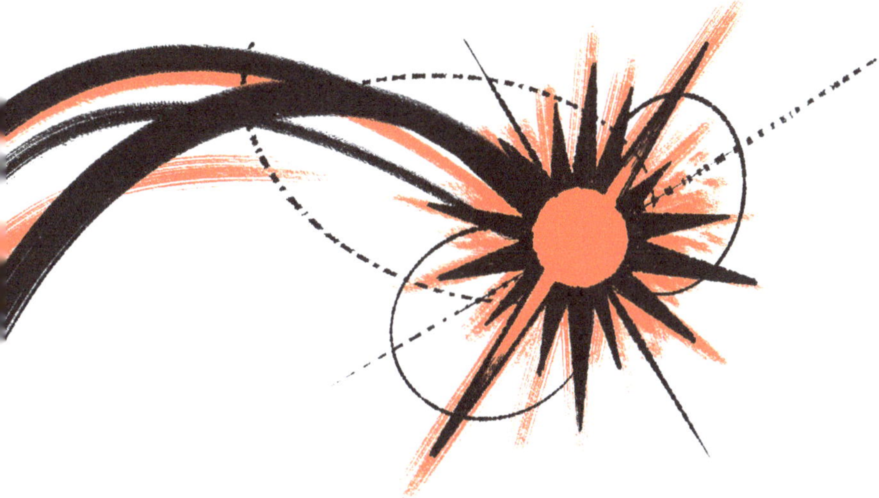

I pushed through the door with a little too much force, instantly drawing the attention of everyone inside. The Early Bird Café was unexpectedly busy, filled with early risers who looked as though they had been awake for hours, preparing for work. Who else would be up at such an ungodly hour? I tried to remember what day it was, but my brain refused to cooperate. Despite the crowd, the café had a warm, cosy atmosphere, and I felt an unexpected sense of comfort. Spotting the only empty table, I made a beeline for it, eager to sink into the soft chair.

I paused, taking in the small, worn table before me. The

faded linoleum surface, scuffed by years of use, stood as a silent witness to countless conversations and passing strangers. Freshly wiped, it still bore faint streaks of moisture. At its centre, the salt and pepper shakers, napkin dispenser, and a jar of mustard were arranged with quiet care. It was a snug little table for two, and as I settled into the chair, my gaze drifted to the park across the street. For the briefest moment, a wave of nostalgia washed over me, carrying with it a glimmer of happiness I hadn't felt in what seemed like forever.

But my thoughts kept returning to Madame Bea, pale as a ghost, practically forcing me from her consulting room. And Eddie, her familiar, with his biting sarcasm. What could possibly have frightened her so badly?

They'll come for you.

The words echoed in my mind, sounding like something from a low-budget horror film. I sighed, trying instead to hold on to the few hopeful things she had told me.

A shadow suddenly fell across the table.

I jumped in my seat, letting out an embarrassingly small yelp.

A tall waitress stood beside me, chewing gum with an almost aggressive determination. One eyebrow arched, clearly unimpressed by my reaction.

'What'll it be, love?' she asked in a nasally voice, the sort that comes from years of blocked sinuses. The gum snapped rhythmically between her teeth, each sharp pop punctuating the silence. She caught me staring.

'Nicotine gum,' she said flatly. 'Tenth time trying to quit.'

'Ah...'

I nodded, attempting an expression of sympathy. My eyes dropped to the plastic name badge pinned to her apron.

Doris.

'I'll have a coffee, please, Doris. And... do you have any chocolate bars? You do? Great. I'll have one of those too.'

She folded her arms and gave me a look of open disapproval.

'That's not your breakfast, is it? You could do with a proper fry-up instead of a chocolate bar.'

She shifted her weight from one foot to the other, judgement dripping from every word.

Feeling like a schoolboy being told off, I hurriedly added,

'Fine... and an orange juice.'

With a theatrical huff, Doris shuffled away towards the kitchen. The smell drifting from within was mouth-watering, but all I really needed was enough caffeine to stop myself collapsing where I sat.

The coffee, orange juice and chocolate bar arrived

quickly.

I took a sip of the hot black coffee and, for a fleeting moment, felt content.

The window beside me slowly fogged over as I stared outside, my thoughts drifting back—not merely to the last few hours, but to the last three years. It had been relentless, and I had reached my breaking point. Cold wind rattled the windows each time the door opened, and the thought of walking back to my car later filled me with dread.

Madame Bea's warnings continued circling my thoughts, leaving far more questions than answers.

What if I really did find her?

How could I possibly explain that I had been her husband in a previous life?

It would terrify anyone.

I buried my face in my hands, staring into the dark depths of my coffee, desperate for clarity. For the first time in years, genuine doubt crept in. The plan had always seemed simple—find her and somehow recognise her among millions of strangers.

But it had always been a terrible plan.

Every encounter filled me with hopeful anticipation before anxiety inevitably took over. I'd stumble through awkward introductions, desperately trying to keep the conversation alive long enough to decide whether I'd finally found her.

But what was I actually searching for?

Would she even resemble the woman I had loved?

I had no idea what she looked like now.

And if I did find her...

then what?

The reality of what I had devoted the last three years of my life to crashed over me all at once.

I slumped back in my chair, staring blankly through the fogged window at the pale, frost-bitten lawn outside.

Perhaps Madame Bea had been right.

Perhaps what I was doing really was unnatural.

I had dredged memories from another lifetime back into the light.

Maybe they had been buried for a reason.

Perhaps the real challenge was learning to forget. To quieten those relentless memories and simply live.

How many meaningful connections had I missed because of this obsession?

In the silence of my thoughts, a quiet voice whispered:

Let go.

Let her go.

At the far end of the café, a shadow lingered.

It had always been there, lurking somewhere at the edge of my thoughts, yet whenever I tried to look directly at it, my eyes slid past as though refusing to focus.

Still...

I could feel it watching me.

Drawing me.

I shook my head.

I was tired.

Tired in the way the Earth must grow weary of endlessly chasing its own shadow around the Sun.

The idea of letting go, of beginning again, suddenly felt almost comforting.

Maybe it really was time.

Maybe it was finally time to live.

I had given everything I had to this search.

With a flicker of quiet determination, I looked around the café, deciding that perhaps today I would simply speak to someone. Anyone.

Then I saw her.

A woman about my age stepped inside, escaping the morning cold. Honey-brown curls tumbled to her shoulders, framing golden-brown skin that seemed to hold its own gentle warmth against the grey dawn. She paused by the door.

Our eyes met.

Something inside her calm brown gaze held me there.

She wore a royal blue jumper, grey jeans tucked into a pair of Dr. Martens, and a bright yellow scarf that swirled softly around her as she moved.

'Do... would you like to sit here?' I stammered, immediately stumbling over my words. 'There aren't any other tables free, and I won't be here long. We could share... if you'd like.'

She looked surprised, taking a cautious half-step backwards.

My heart sank.

Perhaps I'd been too forward.

But then her warm brown eyes met mine again, quietly weighing my intentions.

'Thank you,' she said after a brief pause, smiling gently. 'Sure. That sounds lovely. I usually sit at the table in the corner, but it's occupied.'

She gestured towards the shadowed corner where I now noticed a man slouched in a leather jacket covered in metal studs, his spiked hair standing stiff as a scrubbing brush. Everything about his posture suggested he wasn't interested in company.

'He doesn't seem like the sharing type,' she said with a grin.

It was the most beautiful smile I'd seen in a very long time.

Relief washed through me as she slipped gracefully into the chair opposite.

She chuckled. 'I can tell you don't do this often.'

'I... no, I don't,' I admitted. 'I just decided to be more open. Try to meet new people.'

Her eyebrows lifted. 'So, are you shy, and is your therapist pushing you to reach out? Is that him over there, keeping an eye on you?'

She pointed towards a random stranger.

I laughed. 'No, sorry,' I said, grinning at her offbeat humour. 'I'm not in therapy. I've just recently moved on from someone, and...'

I trailed off, trying not to sound strange.

'I thought that instead of sitting here feeling gloomy, I'd talk to someone and distract myself. Then you walked in, so...'

'...and now we're here,' she said, grinning. 'Not because you were instantly infatuated, right? Because that would be far too soon.'

She flashed me a broad smile, her eyes bright with humour. She seemed to understand exactly what I was going through, as though she had been in my position before. Her confidence and playful banter felt strangely comforting.

'Exactly,' I said, realising I had walked straight into her trap. 'But seriously, you are very attractive, and...'

I sighed, aware that I was floundering.

'I suppose I'm a little rusty when it comes to talking to women. Sorry.'

I offered her a sheepish smile, complete with my best puppy-dog eyes.

She laughed at my awkward expression just as Doris appeared beside us.

'That's funny, love. He's just ordered your usual. Do you two know each other?' she asked, snapping her gum loudly.

We both laughed and shook our heads.

'No,' the woman replied casually, glancing at me with a playful glint in her eye. 'We've only just met. Right?'

She winked, and my heart skipped, though I tried not to show it.

'Right,' I confirmed, looking up at the surly waitress. 'First time.'

When I turned back, the woman was watching me intently, her gaze deeper than I had expected, as though she could see straight through me.

I wasn't sure what to make of it.

Doris tapped her notebook impatiently.

'Well, you look knackered, love. How about ordering some proper food?'

'I've been up all night, walking around Hill and

King's...'

The moment I said it, I regretted it.

Mentioning one of Memphis's roughest districts was a mistake. I watched their expressions change, both of them probably imagining the worst possible reasons for someone to be wandering those streets through the night.

'Oh...' Doris said flatly, as though swallowing something bitter.

I suddenly felt the weight of judgement from around the café, as if the eyes from the empty streets had followed me inside.

'No, no,' I stammered. 'It's not what you think. I wasn't... you know...'

My words failed me, and heat rushed into my face.

'I was doing research. It's a long story.'

Doris rolled her eyes and walked away, muttering under her breath.

'Sophie,' the woman said, offering me her hand with a warm smile.

I shook it and held on for a fraction too long.

'I'm Abe,' I replied, feeling the warmth climb further up my neck. 'Part Jewish, part Portuguese... and a little of something else.'

My attempt at a grin felt awkward.

'You're joking!' Sophie laughed, her eyes lighting up. 'No Jewish roots here, but I'm a mix too. Caribbean father, Persian mother. I thought we'd save family histories until at least the third date, Abe—not our first meeting.'

She laughed at her own joke, pushing the boundaries with effortless ease.

Doris returned and placed Sophie's coffee and chocolate on the table.

'Thanks, Doris,' Sophie said.

I offered Doris a quick smile before turning back to Sophie.

'I'm terrible at small talk,' I admitted. 'Do you live around here?'

'Yes. Born and raised. I moved back after uni.'

'Lower Kensington for me,' I said, beginning to relax.

There was something about her that drew me in, making me forget the heartache I had been drowning in. We exchanged stories about growing up in the city, and before long I was breaking off a piece of chocolate and dipping it into my coffee.

Sophie burst out laughing.

'What? I like the way the coffee melts the chocolate.'

She unwrapped her own bar and snapped off a piece.

'I drink the coffee through the chocolate. Like this.'

She demonstrated, and I followed her lead.

The combination was incredible.

'That's genius,' I laughed. 'I've been doing it wrong all this time.'

Sophie's smile softened, and her eyes became thoughtful.

'It's strange meeting you today. What you said earlier, about moving on from someone... it struck a nerve. My housemate gave me the same speech this morning.'

'You're joking.'

She shook her head, and we sat for a moment in comfortable silence, sipping our coffee.

'This feels right, Abe,' she said quietly. 'Who are you?'

I chuckled and leaned closer.

'I'm a double agent. My mission is to make you interested enough to cover for me while I send classified information to my superiors.'

I gave her a mock salute and nearly knocked over the cups.

'Careful!' Sophie laughed, catching one just in time.

Doris reappeared with a pot of coffee and a knowing smirk.

'Looks like you two could use a refill. On the house.'

She winked and disappeared again, her peculiar charm beginning to grow on me.

'Perfect,' I said, filling our cups.

Sophie glanced at her watch, but neither of us seemed eager to leave.

'I've got a little time,' I said.

'Me too.'

Her enthusiasm was infectious.

We allowed the conversation to flow, moving easily from one subject to the next. We laughed about old films, debated art and science fiction, and exchanged book recommendations. It felt effortless, as though all the weight I had carried into the café had vanished.

As we spoke, I realised how rare it was to feel so comfortable with someone so quickly. Sophie seemed perfect in every way, and for a moment I wondered why I had not allowed myself to do this sooner.

Then it occurred to me.

Had I let go of the past any earlier, I might never have met her.

'Oh no. I have to go or I'll miss my lift,' she said, suddenly checking her watch.

'Where are you going?' I asked as she gathered her things.

'Work. I'm at a studio gallery—an artists' co-operative. We run a space on Woolworth and Barclay. Just a group of friends from school who decided to join forces.'

She handed me a vibrant business card, its colours as warm as her smile.

'This was fun,' she said. 'I didn't expect to go on a date this morning.'

'It did feel like a date,' I agreed, standing with her.

'Will I see you again?' she asked, holding my gaze and sending my pulse racing.

She lingered for a moment.

'What do you do?'

'I write,' I said. 'For magazines and newspapers...'

I didn't want her to leave, but I knew she had to. My heart raced as I hesitated between offering my hand and attempting a hug.

She leaned in first.

I embraced her warmly.

'I'd love to see you again,' I said softly.

'Come and find me, Abe.'

Her smile seemed to illuminate the room.

She turned and walked towards the door, giving me a shy wave before disappearing outside. I could have sworn there was a bounce in her step, and I hoped more than anything that I was the reason for it.

I dropped back into my chair and ran my hands through my hair, scarcely able to believe what had happened.

Then something in the ashtray caught my eye.

My heart stopped.

I carefully lifted a chocolate wrapper from among the ashes and placed it on the table.

It had been tied into a familiar knot.

One I had seen countless times before.

One that belonged to another life.

My wife had tied wrappers
like this, leaving those
small,

looping ribbons scattered around our home.
The memory of the park returned in a rush—the day we had promised there would be a sign.

Was this it?

The wrapper lay before me, perfectly formed in the shape of an infinity symbol.

Tears filled my eyes, sudden and overwhelming. They slipped from the bridge of my nose and splashed onto the table, running down my cheeks and neck.

I looked around the almost empty café, but the world beyond that table had ceased to matter.

I had found her.

I knew her name.

I knew where she worked.

And as I sat there, quietly sobbing into my hands, time seemed to stop.

After three years of searching, just as hope had begun to leave me, I had found her.

The Jackal

Chapter seven

O chacal

The Jackal

'Mind if I sit, mate?' came a grating voice from my right. 'What's got you down, bruv? Feeling a bit blue?'

The thin rasp of his voice made my skin crawl. The hair on the back of my neck bristled, and an involuntary shiver tightened my stomach. Before I even looked up, I knew who was speaking.

I winced and turned towards him, immediately realising that the man standing beside my table was anything but ordinary.

To anyone else, he might have appeared merely strange,

but something about him radiated menace. His eyes were concealed behind pitch-black, eighties-style sunglasses that drew me in like an abyss. I thought I could just make out something moving behind the lenses, though I couldn't be certain. His hair was shaped into a rigid mohawk, accentuating ears that jutted out like malformed flaps of flesh. Piercings covered almost every available inch of his face, which seemed twisted into a permanent sneer.

He was dressed entirely in black leather: steel-reinforced boots, a vintage jacket with the collar raised high around his neck, and rows of spikes and studs lining every seam. He towered over me, a looming monument to aggression and defiance.

'So, what's it gonna be? You gonna invite me to sit, like you did that fit bird, or not?'

His voice dripped with contempt.

Every instinct screamed, **No fucking way.**

But somehow my mouth betrayed me.

'Um... okay,' I said, exhaling slowly as I tried to conceal my fear.

His face brightened, and he dropped heavily into the chair opposite me with a grunt.

'Aw, that's nice,' he said, his voice thick with sarcasm. 'They said you were polite.'

He stared straight through me, as though I were made

of glass.

'So, kid, you got what you wanted, didn't you?'

He shrugged, gesturing vaguely in the direction Sophie had gone.

'So now we're done. That's the deal. You got it, bruv?'

His tone became suddenly formal, and his sneer assumed a disturbingly bureaucratic quality.

'Under specific conditions—where there is perceived unfairness, an unsatisfactory outcome, or a complaint—the applicant may request remedial action from the oversight committee. Blah, blah, blah.'

He smiled, revealing far too many teeth.

'Now,' he growled, his eyes briefly glowing red behind the dark lenses, 'once the so-called "agreement" has concluded'—he made exaggerated quotation marks with his fingers—'some applicants may find themselves dissatisfied with the result.'

He sniffed and leaned back, raising his clawed hands with theatrical ceremony.

'Enter... me.'

He pointed one claw towards his chest.

Through a gap in his leather jacket, I noticed a Ramones T-shirt. I wondered whether he genuinely liked the band or whether it was simply another confusing layer of his presence in the café.

'That's right. Think of me as an enforcer. An upholder of peace and contracts.'

My unease continued to grow.

'Right, then. Any last words? Anything you want me to pass on to the higher-ups? I don't speak directly to the—you know—the Demiurge, but someone'll pass your message along.'

He lowered his sunglasses slightly, allowing me a clearer glimpse of the eyes beneath.

They were feral.

Wild beyond anything that belonged on Earth.

He waited.

My head throbbed, stunned by his sudden appearance. I could barely comprehend what I was hearing.

What the fuck was happening?

'Um... I'm afraid I don't understand. Are you saying I'm going to die? That my time is up?'

A wave of nausea moved through me.

'What?'

He barked out a laugh.

'No, no, son. Don't be that kind of special, all right?'

He leaned closer.

'I'm saying you can't follow the bird. You can't pursue her, speak to her, mate with her—whatever. You found her. Now leave her alone. Got it?'

My jaw must have dropped, because he shrugged.

'Hey, I don't make the rules. I enforce them. If you want to lodge a complaint, you'll have to go through the proper channels.'

He paused.

'And that means dying.'

'But—' I spluttered, forgetting for a moment that I was sitting opposite what appeared to be pain made flesh. 'I don't remember making any deal.'

'Yeah? That's because your subconscious made it, innit? Sorry, bruv. Valid interaction. You should keep a tighter rein on yourself.'

He shot to his feet and pulled up his trousers, adjusting his belt.

'Well.'

He made a long, wet snorting sound as he cleared his sinuses.

'My job's done. Have a happy life. And remember—don't try to see her again, because if I come back, I won't be bringing only my natural charm. I'll bring medicine. Got it?'

I stared at him blankly.

'Not that it matters much. Countdown's already started.'

His face twisted into a vicious snarl.

'Memory reset in twenty-four hours.'

He bent down until his face was inches from mine. His breath smelt of wet dog.

'But before those twenty-four hours are up, motherfucker, don't go getting any fucking ideas.'

He slapped my cheek lightly with his palm.

'Use your brain. Be smart. All right?'

He stood and straightened his jacket.

'And you're welcome, by the way. Good banter, son.'

He strutted down the aisle and out through the door without once looking back.

My head and heart went numb.

Disbelief became denial.

Denial became anger.

Anger became despair.

But it never reached acceptance.

'What the fuck?' I said aloud.

Doris stirred behind the counter.

What was happening?

Reality had flushed itself down the pipes again, just as it had on the day I surfaced and discovered an entire part of myself that had previously been hidden.

Everything had changed once more.

The walls around me seemed to peel away and collapse. The floor gave beneath me.

I leapt up, struck the table with my legs, swore in pain and spilt the remaining coffee across the linoleum surface. Doris raised her eyebrows as she watched me stumble.

I thought I might vomit.

I had to get out.

The café spun around me as I forced myself towards the door. Somehow, my legs carried me outside, where I collapsed onto the cracked pavement and retched violently.

When I finally stood, the thin curtains of reality seemed unstable and translucent. I stared beyond the solid shapes of the world, into the depths behind them, seeing only with the eyes of my imagination.

Something was there.

Multiple fields of energy.

Intelligence I could feel but could not locate.

I registered my complaint with an upward thrust of my middle finger.

'Fuck this! You can't stop me!' I screamed into the void, fury spilling over.

How could I be held accountable for a choice I couldn't

even remember making?

Theorising about the future was nothing like being forced to live it.

How could a decision lead me to the very edge of everything I had ever wanted, only to drag me backwards as I reached for it?

No.

Not after coming this close.

Not while standing within reach of everything I had fought for.

There was no chance in hell I was walking away.

The leather-clad freak had been right about one thing: agreements like this, where a person was forced to surrender what they wanted most, had to be enforced.

But what did I have left to lose?

He had said my memories would be erased in twenty-four hours. His threat had backfired. Instead of frightening me away, it had sharpened my resolve.

Instead of driving me away from Sophie, it drove me towards her.

She was the only thing left that I could still choose.

The final piece of this twisted puzzle that remained within my reach.

No one was going to keep me from her now.

Not when I knew who she was.

Not when I was certain she was the woman I had spent years searching for.

I tightened my fingers around the loop of chocolate wrapper in my hand, tied into a perfect infinity symbol.

She had made it.

Somewhere inside her, some part of her remembered too.

She wanted to be found.

And I would not allow anyone to stop me.

Not now.

Not ever.

81

3321

37	78	29	62	3	54	25	46	17
18	38	79	30	63	4	55	26	47
48	19	39	80	31	64	5	56	27
28	49	20	40	81	32	65	6	57
58	21	50	11	41	82	33	66	7
8	59	22	51	12	42	83	34	67
68	9	60	23	52	13	43	84	35
36	69	10	61	24	53	14	44	85
86	16	70	1	72	15	45	76	67

Part two

CHAMBER OF GLASS

A hidden place of undoing, where forms unmake themselves in light.

Darkness seeps through skin like ink through paper.

The new form hardens, gleams — perfect, terrible.

Above, the others wait.

The chamber hums.

The female stands in stillness, her carapace pulsing with light, her scent thick and electric.

The World

Chapter one

O Mundo Invertida

The World Reversed

That had to be the Jackal.

He radiated the same terror I had felt coming from Madame Bea when she spoke his name. If he was to be believed, I had twenty-four hours before I forgot everything about my past life and all I had discovered since.

I hadn't slept.

I wasn't going to sleep any time soon.

Not if I wanted to see Sophie.

Then, of course, there was the Jackal. I had no doubt he would go to any length to enforce the bargain. He was violence personified, barely contained.

I knew it.

I felt it.

The biting wind sliced through me as I stumbled down the street, a stark reminder that winter had arrived during the early hours of the morning. I pushed into a chemist just as it was opening, passing a woman in a white coat who was meticulously dusting the shelves near the entrance.

Her suspicious gaze lingered on me.

I could only imagine how haggard and dishevelled I looked after the night I had endured, particularly after being sick only moments earlier. I managed a weak smile and scanned the shelves for some chemical burst of energy that might carry me through whatever came next.

I grabbed a packet of pills and an energy drink, paid quickly, then swallowed several tablets with the first mouthful.

The effect struck almost at once, igniting a sharp sense of urgency.

I hurried back towards my car.

It was still early. The clock on the chemist's wall had

read half past seven. That left me with roughly twenty-three hours before the hard reset erased everything I remembered.

Half past six the following morning.

I needed a plan.

Fast.

The roads were growing busier, morning traffic already beginning to thicken. I turned the key, the engine roaring to life, and sped towards the alley where I had found Madame Bea the night before.

In the cold morning light, the city's worn grey buildings seemed exhausted, almost lifeless.

I spotted an empty parking space across from the alley, manoeuvred into it and scrambled from the car, sprinting down the narrow street towards Madame Bea's shop.

The tall buildings loomed overhead, blocking the sunlight and giving me the uneasy sensation of entering a tunnel. The alley seemed to tighten around me, bending and twisting as I moved deeper into it, until I stood once more before the peculiar façade of the tall terraced house wedged between its neighbours.

Breathless, I scanned the street to make certain no one had followed me.

Then I knocked.

I had promised never to return, but everything had

changed.

Even the possibility of having to speak to Edward again could not deter me.

I pounded on the door, frustration rising with every unanswered knock. The neon signs were dark, their glow replaced by a dull grey-blue light filtering down from the narrow strip of sky above.

I knocked again.

Nothing.

Silence pressed heavily around me.

I tried the handle.

To my surprise, it turned.

The door creaked open, releasing a breath of stale air that raised the hairs along my arms. A dark charge seemed to pulse through my skull and down into my hands as I stepped across the threshold.

Something was wrong.

Everything had changed.

Swallowing hard, I moved into the darkness.

The waiting room had been stripped bare. The rug, the benches and the photographs that once covered the walls were gone. My footsteps stirred clouds of dust that could not possibly have settled there since the night before.

The consultation room was empty too.

Dust coated the floor, disturbed only by strange scratches and irregular markings. Delicate paw prints circled through them, as though a cat had wandered restlessly around the outline of a human figure.

I approached the place where the Ottoman had stood.

Four circular impressions remained in the dust.

Confusion tightened my throat as I looked towards the staircase. Grey daylight filtered through the small barred window behind me, stretching my shadow up the steps.

'Hello?' I called. 'It's Abe.'

Only my echo answered.

'Madame Bea? I need your help.'

My voice trembled.

Something shifted in the darkness above.

I froze.

A chill crept slowly up my spine as every muscle in my body tightened. For one absurd moment, I hoped that if I remained perfectly still, whatever was hiding there might fail to notice me.

But it was already too late to retreat.

I drew a breath and stepped closer.

'Madame Bea? Is that you?'

'Don't come any closer,' a ragged voice hissed from above.

I squinted into the darkness.

A hunched figure sat slumped in an ancient rocking chair, wrapped in layers of filthy cloth.

'Is... is that you?' I stammered.

'You promised not to come back,' she growled.

'I'm sorry. I didn't know where else to go. I found her, just as you said I would.'

My eyes adjusted slowly to the gloom. Withered hands gripped the arms of the chair. Beneath the folds of cloth, Madame Bea seemed scarcely more substantial than the shadows around her.

'After I left, a man appeared and told me my time was up. He said I couldn't see her again. That I'd made some kind of bargain and the terms had been fulfilled. Then he threatened me. He said I would forget everything in twenty-four hours.'

I shifted uneasily, and the shadows seemed to flicker in response.

'I think it was the Jackal. What's happening, Madame?'

She remained silent for a long time.

When she finally spoke, her voice crackled from somewhere deep within the bundle of cloth.

'That was the Jackal. He's a ruthless son of a bitch. Don't cross him, Abe. Accept that you have to forget. Forget her. Very few have survived defying him, and the outcomes are never what they hoped for.'

'You survived him, didn't you?' I asked, sensing something unspoken between them.

She released a heavy sigh.

'Can't you leave it alone? When will you learn?'

'What happened to you, Madame? What did he do?'

'I was once in your position,' she admitted, her voice softening. 'So I know what I'm talking about. Go home and forget.'

'Would you have listened?' I challenged. 'Would you have gone home?'

Her silence answered for her.

At last, she said, 'All right. I'll tell you what you need to know.'

She paused.

'You caught me while I was packing. I'm moving on. If the Jackal is prowling around here, I need to disappear quickly. We're no longer on good terms.'

Relief flickered through me, but it did not last.

'Don't thank me, Abe. You're walking into a storm. It won't be pretty.'

She struggled to her feet.

In the half-light, she looked frail, a diminished shadow of the woman I had met only hours earlier.

'The Jackal has the power to pass judgement. If he decides you're not complying, he can take you down in an instant. Don't provoke him unless you're prepared for the consequences. And if you do, make certain you do it properly and get away quickly.'

She moved closer, each step laboured.

'No one has ever killed the Jackal. He isn't alive in the way you understand life.'

Her gaze sharpened.

'Your only way out of one bargain is to make another. You'll have to weave a tangled web of agreements merely to stay afloat. It won't be easy.'

She extended a gnarled hand.

Between her fingers was a tattered card, its surface slick with age.

I took it carefully.

A mesmerising halftone pattern shimmered across one side before fading into dullness on the right, as though the design were trying to escape the paper and settle onto my skin.

At the centre, two words had been elegantly embossed.

Beneath them was a simple, chilling slogan:

Making dreams come true, one soul at a time.

I brought the card closer and finally deciphered the title.

'El Diablo?' I frowned in disbelief. 'The Devil? Seriously?'

I looked up at Madame Bea.

She erupted into a cackle and began limping back up the stairs.

'He's always been a bit of a joker, my friend. If you need to renegotiate your deal, he's your man—at a price, of course. You'll want someone sharp, like a lawyer. He knows his way around these things.'

'I'm not making a deal with the Devil!' I protested, horror creeping into my voice.

'Who else have you got, Abe?' she shot back, irritation creeping into her tone. 'And don't squeeze him into the shape of some holy book. He isn't what you think he is. Remember, nothing is ever as it appears.'

She paused.

'Now I really must be going. The last time I crossed paths with the Jackal, we didn't exactly see eye to eye, and I have no desire to repeat the experience. I rather like it here. This realm suits me just fine.'

She retreated into the shadows.

Panic seized me.

'Wait!' I called. 'How do I find him?'

'Edward,' she gasped, her voice barely above a whisper. 'He'll guide you further. Speak to him on your way out, sweetie.'

A sudden wind swept in behind me, pulling every shadow in the room with it. They spiralled up the staircase into a dark vortex around her.

Seconds later...

she was gone.

The oppressive darkness vanished with her.

I turned the card over in my hands several times before slipping it into my pocket.

The alley somehow felt lighter as I hurried back towards my car.

Perched on the bonnet like a king upon a metallic throne sat Edward.

'What the hell, Abe! Didn't I tell you to leave Bea alone?'

He practically spat the words at me.

'Stop being an arsehole, Ed!' I snapped back. 'Madame says you can help me find the Devil. Just give me the facts and I'll be on my way.'

The familiar snorted, his whiskers twitching with disdain.

For a long moment, he simply stared at me.

Finally, he sighed.

'Fine. Drive north out of the city on the old national road. Keep going into the desert. Stay on the main road through the wasteland. You'll need to find Prince first.'

He scratched absent-mindedly behind one ear.

'Well... technically, Prince finds you.'

He pointed one furry finger at me.

'It helps if you're lost.'

Another pause.

'Or desperate.'

He shrugged.

'Prince turns up when people need him. Once he finds you, ask him to take you to the Devil.'

A crooked grin spread across his face.

'Good luck.'

And just like that...

he disappeared.

The air suddenly felt colder, as though winter itself had quietly announced its arrival.

I turned my collar against the biting wind and climbed into the driver's seat.

Taking the card from my pocket once more, I studied it beneath the pale daylight.

Childhood memories of the Devil surfaced uninvited.

None of them were particularly pleasant.

I certainly hadn't imagined that one day I'd be setting out to find him in the hope of solving my problems.

'Fuck it,' I muttered.

I turned the key.

The engine growled into life.

Pulling onto the road, I pointed the car towards the commercial district.

With less than twenty hours remaining, I was determined to see Sophie one more time.

Yet the memory of the Jackal lingered heavily in my thoughts.

Madame Bea's warning echoed in my mind.

If a confrontation became inevitable...

I had to be ready.

A bitter laugh escaped me.

Surely it wouldn't come to that.

I still believed I could reason with the Jackal.

Surely I could make him understand.

The Tower

Chapter two

A Torre

The Tower

Despite the biting wind and bitter cold, it was turning into a beautiful day. The sky stretched overhead in an ethereal blue, and a strange calm settled over me as I navigated the streets towards Sophie. Her studio—a vibrant creative space she shared with fellow artists—was nestled in one of the liveliest parts of the city. I knew she'd be there, immersed in preparations for the exhibition she had mentioned that morning, the very reason she'd been out of bed before dawn.

The commercial district pulsed with energy, its towering glass buildings standing in sharp contrast to the older classical architecture that surrounded them. Sophie's studio occupied a prime position within Gilbert Tower, at the bustling corner of Woolworth and Barclay. The area assaulted the senses with neon lights, giant billboards and flickering television screens all competing for attention. Studio Seventy-Two stood apart, its striking black and brown façade framed by reclaimed timber and broad glass doors fashioned from salvaged materials of another era. Inside, the gallery showcased exceptional fine art for discerning collectors and an affluent clientele.

On the second floor, expansive studios were flooded with sunlight pouring through towering windows overlooking the frenetic streets below. Golden light animated the stately stone façade of Gilbert Tower. At its base, the collective's thriving gallery dominated the corner—a signature work by one of the city's celebrated architects at the height of his career. The postmodern tower rose fifty-seven storeys into the skyline, crowned by an extravagant penthouse. Luxury apartments occupied the upper floors, while the lower two housed commercial spaces. Around Studio Seventy-Two clustered elegant cafés, independent bookshops and carefully curated boutiques.

Yet the studio remained the heart of the block.

I knew the area well.

I'd spent years working around the corner for a local magazine.

By the time I reached Woolworth and Barclay, the

morning rush was in full swing. Fortune favoured me, and I found a parking space only a block away. As I walked towards the studio, I stopped beside a newsstand, my heart pounding as my eyes searched the second-floor windows, hoping—aching—for a glimpse of Sophie.

The urge to run straight across the road and burst inside almost overwhelmed me.

Only the thinnest thread of reason held me back.

No sign of the Jackal.

A cold wave of dread swept over me as I stared at the studio's broad glass doors. They stood like silent sentinels, dark and forbidding, warning me away without uttering a word.

I turned aside, pressing my clenched fists against my temples and staring at the pavement beneath my feet.

My nerves were stretched taut, suspended between retreat and resolve.

Behind me, the newspapers seemed to cry out in protest.

STOP.

DON'T GO.

They referred to some political scandal, yet every headline felt directed at me. I sensed the Jackal in every bold letter, like static prickling through the air.

My breath clouded before me.

The crowd drifted past like a river.

Then I turned back.

Tunnel vision narrowed the world to those doors.

Each step felt impossibly slow.

My pale, trembling hand closed around the steel handle.

Every instinct screamed at me to stop.

Still...

I pulled.

The door swung open.

I stepped into the hushed reception of Gilbert Tower.

Minimalist.

Cold.

The foyer lay steeped in shadow: slate-blue floors, exposed concrete walls broken by stained diagonal timber panels, stainless steel trims cutting hard lines through the space.

Compared with the chaos outside, the silence felt unnatural.

A sleek sign pointed towards the rich mahogany doors of Studio Seventy-Two.

Warm light spilled through their glass panels like a beacon.

I wanted to walk towards it.

Instead, my legs locked.

My body lurched sideways, staggering like a sailor caught in a storm. I stumbled across the empty lobby before collapsing against the cold doors of a lift opposite the studio.

With a soft hiss, they slid open behind me.

I fell backwards inside.

The Jackal was waiting.

Smiling.

I writhed helplessly across the floor of the lift like a fish flung onto a deck, struggling to stand but managing only to spin clumsily in a slow circle. Drool slipped from the corner of my mouth.

My eyes found his.

Red.

Bright.

Amused.

The doors closed.

We were alone.

He raised a gloved fist and slammed it against the control panel.

The lift lurched upwards.

'Ahh, mate,' he grinned, baring teeth like broken knives. 'Had a feeling you'd turn up. Knew you wouldn't play along... so I arranged a little surprise. Something special, bruv.'

His eyes glittered.

He was enjoying every second.

'See, I thought to myself—this one's got bollocks. Big swinging ones.'

He straightened, towering above me.

'And I respect that. Honestly, I do. So I'm giving you one last chance.'

He smiled again.

'But trust me... it's completely pointless trying to beat me. You'll work that out soon enough.'

The lift shuddered to a halt.

The Jackal bent down, grabbed the back of my neck and lifted me as effortlessly as though I were made of straw.

'There's a bloke up on fifty-five,' he said conversationally as he dragged me along the corridor. 'An idiot. Just like you. Wouldn't respect the limits of his little agreement with the oversight committee. I warned him, bruv. Fair and square. But the fool wouldn't listen.'

He shrugged.

'So now... we have to have the end-of-the-line conversation.'

He planted me in front of the final door along the corridor.

The dizziness began to fade, replaced by something colder.

Fear.

Real fear.

The Jackal knocked.

Three deliberate raps.

'Benji!' he barked.

Movement stirred beyond the door.

Fear seeped through the walls.

Then—

Crash.

One kick.

The door exploded inwards.

Light flooded the corridor.

I threw an arm across my eyes.

Inside stood a short, balding man with a thin moustache, shaking uncontrollably. He gripped a revolver in both hands, arms locked rigid, eyes wide with panic.

'Die! Die, you fucking dog!' he screamed.

He fired.

Again.

Again.

Again.

Bullets tore through the hallway, splintering wood and

blasting chunks of concrete from the walls.

One grazed my cheek.

'Jesus Christ!' I shouted, clutching my face.

The Jackal never even flinched.

He simply stood there.

Watching.

Sneering.

'Benji... Benji...'

He sighed, brushing dust from his jacket while the revolver clicked empty.

Benji's trembling fingers fumbled desperately with fresh rounds.

Half of them spilled onto the floor.

'You injured my guest, mate.'

The Jackal shook his head.

'That's rude, innit?'

He stepped calmly into the flat.

In one effortless movement, he took the revolver, seized Benji by the throat and lifted him clean off the floor.

Then he looked back at me.

Grinning.

'Come here, bruv.'

Blood trickled down my face as I stumbled forwards.

The Jackal held Benji aloft like a rag doll.

'I warned him,' he said. 'Plenty of times.'

He looked almost disappointed.

'And now... look what's happened.'

A dark stain spread across Benji's trousers.

The Jackal carried him towards the balcony.

'Time's up.'

With a screech of glass, the Jackal flung open the sliding doors and stepped out onto the balcony, holding the gasping man over the edge.

Fifty-five storeys up.

'No!' I shouted, rushing towards him. 'Don't!'

The Jackal looked at me as though I were hopelessly naïve.

'What's done is done, bruv. This is the reset. He had his chance.'

His fingers loosened.

'Any last words, Benji?'

Benji, pale but defiant, lifted his eyes to mine.

'Don't listen to him,' he croaked. 'I regret... nothing.'

The Jackal released him before he could finish.

Benji disappeared.

'Oops,' the Jackal sneered. 'Wrong message.'

I lurched towards the balcony, reaching out instinctively.

Too late.

He was already a tiny figure tumbling towards the street below.

A heartbeat later came the dull, sickening crunch.

Then a car alarm began wailing.

I collapsed against the balcony rail, trembling.

The Jackal leaned lazily against the wall, looking thoroughly satisfied.

'You get the picture now, son?' he asked, clapping me on the shoulder. 'We're going back downstairs nice and quiet, yeah? You walk away. No fuss.'

I turned from him.

The flat was in ruins.

The revolver still lay where he had casually dropped it.

My heart pounded.

This was the lesson.

Forget Sophie.

Forget everything.

Walk away.

'Okay,' I said quietly, wiping the tears from my face. 'You win. I'll go home.'

'Good lad,' he replied, sounding almost disappointed.

I stepped towards the open doors, moving quickly.

Behind me, I heard him still talking.

'I thought you'd be more of a problem. But look at ya... finally got some sense.'

I didn't think.

I couldn't.

In two strides I reached the revolver.

My hand closed around the grip.

I spun.

Screaming, I pulled the trigger.

Again.

Again.

Again.

The bullets slammed into him.

Chest.

Shoulder.

Neck.

Blood sprayed across the balcony.

For the first time...

his sneer disappeared.

I threw myself at him, driving my shoulder into his chest.

The final shot rang out.

The chamber clicked empty.

I brought the revolver crashing into his face.

Once.

Twice.

Again.

He staggered backwards.

His clawed hands reached desperately for me.

One final strike.

Then he toppled over the balcony rail.

Gone.

I watched him fall for only a second.

Then I staggered backwards, collapsed against the wall and slid to the floor, shaking so violently I could barely breathe.

What had I done?

Had I finally lost my mind?

There was no going back now.

he Tower

Chapter three

A Torre Invertida

The Tower Reversed

Sirens howled from the street below. From where I leaned against the balcony railing, I could already see a crowd beginning to gather.

Once, as a child, I'd been caught in a powerful undertow that had almost dragged me out to sea.

The same panic gripped me now.

That absolute loss of control.

That sickening certainty that things could only end badly.

My head throbbed with a brutal ache, as though nine-inch nails were being hammered through thin timber.

Whatever had actually happened during the last thirty minutes—since the Jackal had kicked Benjamin's front door off its hinges—was never going to be the version the police believed.

It looked bad.

I knew it.

I had to run.

Now.

Run for your fucking life.

My body agreed.

But reason—my oldest tormentor—kept interfering, searching for a sensible middle ground where none existed.

My fingerprints were everywhere.

Certainly all over the revolver.

There wasn't a single witness who could testify that I hadn't wanted everything that had happened.

Christ.

I'd filled the Jackal with bullets.

Then I'd smashed his face with the same gun before sending him over the balcony.

Fifty-five floors down.

Now there were two bodies lying on Barclay Street.

Both demanding an explanation.

Still dazed, I staggered away from the balcony.

There was no version of events that ended well if I stayed.

If I ran...

perhaps they would never know I'd been there.

Forensics might eventually uncover someone else's presence, but it would take time to connect it to me.

A fragile spark of hope flickered.

Terror was already waiting to extinguish it.

As my breathing slowly steadied, the high-pitched ringing in my ears became more noticeable.

Probably burst something during the gunfire.

I tested my legs.

They trembled but obeyed, carrying me towards the shattered front door.

The corridor beyond lay unnaturally silent.

Perhaps everyone else was hiding inside their expensive apartments, determined not to become involved.

I ran for the stairwell.

Predictable?

Probably.

But what choice did I have?

I looked guilty as hell, blood still speckled across my face and neck.

The stairs were deserted.

A stale smell drifted upwards through the centre of the building.

I descended quickly, stopping every few flights to listen for footsteps or voices below.

Eventually I reached the second floor.

Breath ragged.

Body aching.

I eased open the fire door just enough to peer through the gap.

Directly opposite stood the service entrance to Studio Seventy-Two.

If I could just reach Sophie...

perhaps some part of this nightmare would begin to make sense.

The corridor was empty.

Heart hammering, I slipped through.

A short passage led to a lift lobby washed in flashing blue reflections from the emergency vehicles outside.

A faint electrical hum vibrated through the building.

My legs weakened as I imagined what was happening below.

I ducked into the nearby public toilets to gather myself.

The cubicles were empty.

Good.

The mirror above the sinks reflected a stranger.

Pale skin.

Wild eyes.

I washed the blood from my face, dried myself with paper towels and stared at my reflection.

How had it come to this?

The cut along my cheek proved surprisingly shallow once cleaned.

I drew a long breath.

Grounded myself.

Then stepped back into the corridor and headed towards Studio Seventy-Two.

Several wooden frames leaned against the wall beside the entrance.

Above the door hung a simple black-and-white sign.

I tried the handle.

It turned.

I slipped inside.

It didn't feel like a public gallery.

It felt like backstage at a theatre.

Canvases filled every available corner, some blank, others alive with thick brushstrokes. Paint flecked the parquet floor. Doors lined the corridor, leading towards a large window flooded with natural light.

Sophie had said it was a shared studio.

A collective.

The smell reached me first.

Incense.

Turpentine.

Fresh oil paint.

All layered together.

Halfway along stood a coffee machine and water cooler, almost like quiet shrines.

I peered into the first room.

Storage.

No windows.

Only shelves.

The next studio was exactly as I'd imagined.

Huge timber-framed windows.

Several easels displaying intricate half-finished paintings.

The smell of oil paint hung heavily in the air.

A steaming mug of coffee rested on a nearby table beside several chocolate wrappers tied into tiny infinity loops.

Paintings and posters almost completely concealed the faded Victorian wallpaper.

Paint-spattered coats hung from whimsical hooks shaped like dragons and flowers.

Drawn almost instinctively, I wandered towards the window.

Below, Barclay Street had become strangely still.

Traffic stood frozen.

A crowd surrounded a crushed car.

Even from this height I couldn't tell who lay across its roof.

Benjamin?

The Jackal?

Both?

A wave of nausea rolled through me.

I lowered my head into my hands, remorse flooding every part of me.

I wasn't a murderer.

'Abe?'

I spun around.

Sophie stood in the doorway, her paint-spattered coat thrown over her clothes.

She looked exactly the same.

Yet somehow...

everything had changed.

'Wow,' she said. 'What a weird morning. Did you see what happened outside? It's crazy.'

'Outside? Uh... yeah. What's going on?' I asked, trying to sound casual.

She stepped beside me and pointed towards the street.

'Suicide. A man jumped from one of the upper floors. Landed on my friend's car. Hit it so hard he completely crushed the roof.'

I nodded, pretending to absorb the news.

We stood quietly for a moment.

'And the other man?' I asked carefully.

She frowned.

'Huh? What other man?'

'No... I mean... was it definitely just one?'

She smiled.

'Double suicides aren't exactly common. I'm pretty sure I'd have noticed another body.'

She laughed softly before shivering.

Then her expression became thoughtful.

'What do you think makes someone do something like that?' she asked quietly. 'It's such an extreme thing.'

Her eyes drifted back towards the street.

'Do you think we ever see the people we've lost again? After we die?'

The words struck me like a blow.

For a heartbeat I was back in the park.

Back before the war.

Back before everything.

Time folded in upon itself.

I swallowed.

'I think we do come back,' I said quietly. 'I never believed any of it before... but five years ago everything changed. I think we find the people we once loved again.'

I paused.

'Somewhere.'

She watched me carefully.

I turned back towards the window.

'You're certain nothing else happened down there?'

She laughed.

'Nothing else happened, okay? Do you want to go downstairs? I'll come with you.'

I didn't answer.

The Jackal returned to my thoughts.

Could he really die?

Probably not.

Which meant I was living on borrowed time.

For all I knew, he was already climbing the stairs.

Sophie gently touched my arm.

I flinched.

'No... I'm okay,' I said with an awkward laugh. 'I think I imagined two people. Morbid, isn't it?'

The coffee sat steaming beside the familiar infinity loops.

I looked into her deep mahogany eyes.

The moment stretched between us, reaching across lifetimes.

I had found her again.

There was no turning back.

'We've had a strange morning,' I said. 'You're probably wondering whether it could possibly get any stranger.'

I rubbed my forehead.

'There's something I need to tell you.'

I hesitated.

'Something that's really going to top it all.'

She offered a nervous smile.

'About thirty minutes ago...'

I swallowed.

'I met the man who jumped.'

Another pause.

'I met him just before he landed on your friend's car.'

Confusion spread slowly across her face.

I couldn't stop now.

There wasn't enough time.

Strength

Chapter four

Força

Strength

I had to make her understand.

I exhaled and doubled over.

'Abe? Are you okay?'

Her voice wavered as Sophie placed a hand gently on my shoulder.

The truth was, I felt exhausted.

But I couldn't let it show.

I took several slow breaths before forcing myself to speak.

'Look... you say there's only one body out there.'

I glanced towards the window.

'Which means he's coming back.'

I looked directly into her eyes.

'He's coming back for me.'

She searched my face, trying to make sense of what she was hearing.

'You're saying the man outside—the one who jumped—you met him before he died?'

She frowned.

'Oh my God, Abe... that's awful. You knew him?'

'No.'

I rubbed my face, wincing as my fingers brushed the cut on my cheek.

'No, I didn't know him. I saw what happened.'

I swallowed.

'He didn't jump, Sophie.'

Silence settled between us.

'A man... a complete psychopath... threw him from the balcony.'

'He was murdered?'

Her hands flew to her mouth.

I nodded.

'The psychopath calls himself the Jackal. He dragged me upstairs to teach me a lesson. Benjamin... the man outside... was supposed to be an example.'

I hesitated.

There was no avoiding it now.

'An example of what would happen to me... if I didn't leave you alone.'

'Sorry?'

Her confusion deepened.

I rubbed my forehead, desperately trying to think.

'He murdered that man because he didn't want you to see me?'

'Yes... and no.'

I sighed heavily.

'It's more complicated than that. I need you to listen. I know how impossible this sounds, and I know you'll probably think I've lost my mind... but please believe me.'

I took another breath.

'I'm not mad. I swear to you.'

She instinctively took half a step backwards, unsettled by the urgency in my voice.

I immediately regretted frightening her.

'Okay...'

I forced myself to slow down.

'The Jackal found me in the café after you left. He warned me not to come and see you again.'

I looked down at my hands.

'I ignored him.'

Another pause.

'When I arrived here, he was waiting for me.'

I could still see it.

'Benjamin was never the target.'

I met her eyes.

'I was.'

'He threw Benjamin from the building to frighten me.'

I swallowed.

'I tried to stop him.'

The memory burned through me.

'I grabbed Benjamin's revolver...'

The words caught in my throat.

'...and I shot the Jackal.'

She simply stared at me.

No anger.

No interruption.

Only complete stillness.

‘I shot him.’

I laughed once—a hollow, disbelieving sound.

‘I watched him go over the edge.’

I looked towards the window.

‘But you say he isn’t down there.’

Realisation slowly spread through me.

‘Of course he isn’t.’

I shook my head.

‘I was so stupid.’

Sophie gave a short, incredulous laugh.

‘You’re telling me you shot someone off the fiftieth floor... and it makes perfect sense that he isn’t lying in the street?’

I couldn’t even blame her.

‘Yes.’

I nodded.

‘Because the Jackal isn’t human.’

The sentence sounded ridiculous even to me.

‘He’s... something else.’

I searched hopelessly for words.

‘Some kind of entity. A guardian. An enforcer. Something that keeps people inside the boundaries of this reality.’

I gave a helpless shrug.

'Which means he can't be killed.'

Every sentence seemed to bury me a little deeper.

Sophie walked quietly past me, picked up her coffee and took a long drink before turning back.

'Why?'

Her voice was calm.

'Why did he tell you that you couldn't see me again?'

I saw it then.

She was trying to smile.

Trying to stay kind.

But she was frightened.

Of everything I was saying.

Perhaps...

of me.

'This is the hardest part.'

I rubbed my eyes.

'You're going to find it impossible to believe.'

'Try me.'

She smiled nervously.

'I remember my previous life.'

The words hung between us.

'Lots of people say that,' she replied quietly, almost thinking aloud. 'People write books about it.'

'It isn't like that.'

I shook my head.

'I remember everything.'

I looked beyond her, seeing somewhere else entirely.

'Every day. Every conversation. Every moment.'

My voice softened.

'Five years ago... something happened to me.'

'I woke up.'

'I don't know how else to explain it.'

'It felt like surfacing after spending my whole life underwater. As though I'd been sleepwalking until that moment.'

I looked back at her.

'Ever since then, I've been searching for someone.'

I smiled sadly.

'Because I made her a promise.'

There was no gentler way to say it.

I stepped into the truth.

'It was you.'

Silence.

'I promised I'd find you, Sophie.'

My voice barely rose above a whisper.

'I've spent five years searching for you.'

'I found you yesterday morning.'

'I know how unbelievable this sounds.'

I swallowed.

'And I can explain everything.'

A bitter smile crossed my face.

'I'm just not sure we have enough time.'

'Whoa...'

She lifted both hands.

'Just... wait.'

She shook her head slowly.

'You think we knew each other in another life?'

'Not just knew each other.'

I felt tears threatening again.

'We were married.'

The words landed heavily.

'Before I died... you made me promise I'd find you in our next life.'

I couldn't stop now.

'So I searched.'

'I found you.'

'And then the Jackal told me I wasn't allowed to speak to you because of some bargain I apparently made.'

I lowered my head.

Emotion broke through every defence I'd built over the last five years.

'So... for whatever it's worth... I'm sorry if all of this is frightening you.'

I looked at her one last time.

'But you asked me to find you.'

'I kept my promise.'

A tear escaped before I could stop it.

'I loved you.'

A long pause.

'I still do.'

'I'm sorry.'

Sophie leaned silently against her workbench.

Her jaw had fallen open.

She looked completely overwhelmed.

I braced myself.

'Wow...'

She gave a short, incredulous laugh.

'That's probably the most romantic thing I've ever heard.'

She smiled, but there was a sharp edge beneath it.

'Across time... a man finds me to declare his undying love.'

Another bitter laugh escaped her.

She shook her head.

'You do realise I don't remember any of this, right? I don't remember a past life. I didn't even know who you were until this morning.'

Her voice hardened.

'You didn't know me until this morning either.'

The smile disappeared.

'I think you need to leave.'

Her knuckles whitened around the coffee cup.

For a moment I thought she was going to throw it at me.

'You didn't honestly expect me to believe a story like this, did you?'

She looked genuinely distressed now.

'Do you know what's really awful?'

She laughed again, though there wasn't any humour left.

'I've been thinking about you all morning.'

The words hit me harder than I expected.

'I kept thinking... what a lovely guy. I hope he gets in touch.'

She threw her hands into the air.

'Brilliant. Why do I always attract the weird ones?'

Her palms slammed onto the table.

'There *was* something about you.'

She looked almost angry with herself.

'I felt drawn to you.'

Her voice cracked.

'But this...'

She shook her head.

'This is insane.'

She stared directly at me.

'You tell me we were married in another life... that I asked you to find me...'

She swallowed.

'Just leave me alone, okay?'

Colour had rushed into her cheeks.

She was furious.

'There's a man chasing you because he doesn't want us speaking.'

She pointed towards the window.

'There's a dead man lying on my friend's car because he was murdered to make an example of you.'

She stepped backwards.

'Just go.'

Her voice rose.

'Get the fuck out!'

Retreating behind the workbench, she reached into her bag.

Pepper spray.

That was my first thought.

Or something to defend herself.

I couldn't blame her.

I sounded completely insane.

I had backed myself into a corner.

There was nothing left to say.

Devastated, I turned towards the door.

I would have left.

I would never have returned.

But someone was already standing there.

A tall figure leaned casually within the open doorway, blocking my escape.

Ice crawled the length of my spine.

Those familiar red eyes burned into mine.

The Jackal.

Panic exploded inside me.

I searched desperately for another exit.

There wasn't one.

'Oi, oi, oi...'

He pushed himself away from the doorframe.

'Abey... my wayward son.'

His grin widened.

'You look like death.'

He laughed.

'That should be my look, shouldn't it?'

He swaggered into the studio with the easy confidence of a man who had never feared another living thing.

'Ah... and there's Sophie.'

He acknowledged her with a brief nod before dismissing her completely.

'Looks like we've got ourselves a little situation, bruv.'

His smile stretched impossibly wide, revealing too many teeth.

He pointed at Sophie.

'I told you not to come here.'

Then at me.

'Not to *her*, son.'

He burst into laughter.

'But it always happens, doesn't it?'

He slapped both thighs.

'Especially when there's a bit of pussy involved.'

He wiped imaginary tears from his eyes.

'You blokes just can't help yourselves.'

He turned towards Sophie and gave an exaggerated shrug.

'Sorry, love. Didn't mean to be rude.'

A beat.

'Actually... that's a lie.'

His grin returned.

'Now look what you've done, Abey.'

He wagged a finger at me.

'Bad boy.'

He sighed dramatically.

'Now I'll have to erase *her* memory as well.'

His expression darkened.

'But you and me...'

He adjusted his belt.

'We've got unfinished business.'

He leaned closer.

'I reckon you were trying to kill me back on the fifty-fifth floor.'

He shook his head.

'Not very neighbourly.'

His grin returned.

‘Lucky for me, every now and then, when one of my little charges gets the better of me...’

He spread his hands theatrically.

‘...I’ve got a trick.’

He winked.

‘My body melts away.’

He paused.

‘About forty minutes later...’

He tapped his chest.

‘I put myself back together.’

Another grin.

‘Atom by atom.’

He tilted his head.

‘Pretty cool, eh?’

‘I’m sorry,’ Sophie said, stepping from behind her table.

Her voice trembled despite the anger behind it.

‘Who the fuck are you... and who invited you into my studio?’

She glanced sideways at me.

Only for a second.

But it was enough.

Something had changed.

She believed at least part of what I'd told her.

The Jackal laughed directly in her face.

Conflict delighted him.

Without warning he spun.

His fist crashed into mine.

The impact lifted me completely off my feet.

I slammed into the wall with a sickening crack before collapsing in a heap, barely conscious.

Pain exploded through my skull.

Sophie screamed.

The Jackal turned on her.

One brutal backhand.

She flew backwards over the table and crashed onto the floor behind it, her legs kicking helplessly into the air.

I groaned, trying to stand.

Every movement sent pain racing through my spine.

Before I could reach my knees, his shadow swallowed me.

He pinned me beneath one leg and began driving his fists into my head and chest.

His strength was monstrous.

Each blow reverberated through my body like an earthquake.

I pushed against him with everything I had.

He didn't move.

Not even an inch.

Then I understood.

He wasn't trying to hurt me.

He was trying to kill me.

My face throbbed.

I could feel it swelling.

Splitting.

Bleeding.

'I'm gonna teach you a lesson, son!'

Another punch.

'You think you can do whatever you bloody well like?'

Another.

'Fuck all that free-will bollocks, bruv!'

Another.

'When we say no...'

His knee crushed my head against the wall.

'...you say no!'

His fist crashed into my face again.

Through the blur of pain I caught sight of Sophie.

She was crawling.

Slowly.

Towards the doorway.

Good.

She was getting away.

Relief washed over me.

I stopped fighting.

Let my body sink into the floor.

Almost immediately the Jackal stood.

He stepped backwards, breathing heavily as he watched me collapse.

'What?'

He sneered.

'That's it?'

He shook his head.

'I expected better from you, Abe.'

He gestured towards my broken body.

'Look at you.'

A pause.

'Worth it?'

He smiled.

'You should've stayed away.'

Another pause.

'You got your one conversation.'

'That was the deal.'

Blood ran into my eyes.

I wiped it away and looked up through swollen eyelids.

He stood over me, tongue sliding across rows of razor-sharp teeth.

Enjoying every second.

I shook my head.

My body was broken.

But I wasn't.

I regretted nothing.

I tried to speak.

Only a rasp escaped.

'What was that, Abey?'

He leaned closer.

'Trying to say something?'

He wanted to see me empty.

Defeated.

He raised his fist.

Then—

Crack.

A deafening impact echoed through the studio.

I braced for the blow.

It never came.

Several seconds passed before I realised...

he hadn't hit me.

The Jackal staggered forward.

Behind him stood Sophie.

Both hands gripped a heavy length of timber from the studio.

She swung again.

Another crack.

Again.

Again.

Each blow smashed into the back of his skull with a fury I never imagined she possessed.

He never even saw her coming.

She kept striking him...

until he stopped moving.

When it was over, Sophie let the makeshift weapon slip from her hands. It struck the floor with a heavy clang before she dropped down beside me, struggling to catch her breath.

'You okay?' she asked, brushing the blood from my face with trembling fingers.

I nodded.

Or at least I tried to.

'You?'

She shook her head.

'I've been better.'

I reached for her arm, wincing as pain shot through my ribs.

'Thanks for saving me.'

She gave a hollow laugh.

'Strangest day of my life.'

I gestured weakly towards the Jackal's crumpled body behind her.

Its outline was already beginning to fade.

Her eyes widened.

'Oh, shit...'

She turned fully towards it.

'No.'

Her voice became little more than a whisper.

'This isn't happening.'

'He told me he can rebuild himself,' I said. 'Forty minutes.'

'Then we're not waiting around.'

Her voice hardened.

'Your car's across the street, isn't it?'

I nodded.

'Then we leave. Now.'

She looked pale.

The shock hadn't fully reached her yet.

Killing someone—human or otherwise—wasn't something you simply walked away from.

Together we hauled ourselves upright.

Sophie limped back to her workbench, sweeping supplies into a shoulder bag with hurried movements. She dampened the corner of a cloth and gently wiped the blood from my face.

It stung like hell.

But it helped.

'Forty minutes,' she whispered, meeting my eyes.

Something had changed.

There was still fear there.

But behind it...

something else.

Recognition.

'I'm sorry,' I said quietly. 'I never meant to drag you into this. I only wanted to keep a promise.'

I lowered my eyes.

'I loved you, Sophie.'

A pause.

'I still do.'

'I can't help that.'

She remained silent for several moments.

Then she sighed.

'You can't blame me for not believing you.'

'I don't.'

I managed a faint smile.

'To be honest… I'm still not sure what I believe.'

Together we slipped into the corridor.

My skin burned.

My face throbbed.

Every step hurt.

The staircase carried us down into the gallery below.

It was immaculate.

Polished floors.

Perfect lighting.

Paintings and sculptures carefully arranged beneath warm spotlights.

Nothing suggested the violence that had erupted only one floor above.

Near the entrance, several of Sophie's friends stood together discussing the man who had supposedly jumped.

They barely glanced at us.

'See you later,' Sophie called as she steadied me. 'My friend had a little accident. I'm taking him to hospital.'

No one questioned it.

The foyer felt even colder than before.

We pushed through the revolving doors onto the pavement.

Above us, the sky remained impossibly blue.

So peaceful...

it almost felt insulting.

We moved through the gathering crowd towards the road.

Barely ten minutes had passed since the Jackal dissolved.

For all I knew...

he was already rebuilding himself upstairs.

We had to keep moving.

He wasn't the sort of thing that gave up.

I wasn't even sure he could.

We limped together, arms around one another, until we reached my car.

Sophie let out a small laugh.

'I haven't seen one of these in years.'

It was an ageing red Mini Cooper.

I opened the passenger door and almost fell inside.

My body was too battered to drive.

Without hesitation, Sophie slid behind the wheel, started the engine and pulled us away from the kerb.

As we rolled into the street, I glanced back.

A figure stood motionless behind one of the second-floor windows.

Watching us.

It hadn't been forty minutes.

'Drive!' I shouted.

'Sophie... now!'

She didn't hesitate.

Her foot buried the accelerator.

The city dissolved into a blur.

I guided her through unfamiliar streets, directing us towards the outskirts.

I knew where we had to go.

The Karee Desert.

Madame Bea had mentioned the old motorway that crossed it.

Whether it would offer safety...

I had no idea.

Perhaps nowhere could.

But if we could steal a little time—

Time to think.

Time to breathe.

Time to understand who I was...

what the Jackal really was...

and what Sophie and I had become...

Then perhaps—

just perhaps—

we still had a chance.

The Moon

Chapter five

A Lua Invertida

The Moon

I still had seventeen hours before my twenty-four-hour deadline expired.

Not that it felt like it mattered any more.

I'd already broken the rules.

Like a parolee on the run, hunted by some self-appointed afterlife judge, jury and executioner.

By midday, we reached The Roadside American Diner and Drive-Through—a gleaming relic of Americana perched in the middle of nowhere on the N5.

Surrounded by miles of scorched emptiness, the place stood alone, proud and defiant against the endless horizon. Locals and lorry drivers simply called it **The RAD**. It was the last place to find food or fuel before the long, punishing journey north into the Karee Desert.

National Road 5 was one of only a handful of routes leading out of Memphis, but few people travelled it willingly. The Karee was one of the hottest deserts on the planet—brutal, godless, and almost completely empty. Beyond the RAD, the road stretched unbroken through a dead zone with no petrol stations, no rest stops, and no second chances. Even at full speed, it took more than a day to cross. If you broke down out there, you simply didn't come back.

The newer motorways, built decades after the city outgrew its original boundaries, skirted the desert instead. They were safer, smoother and better maintained.

Road 5 had been left to the desperate and the damned.

Overloaded freight lorries.

Smugglers.

Ghosts of the road.

Almost nobody drove the old route any more.

But Sophie and I weren't exactly thinking rationally.

The RAD had always been a place of comfort for me—a polished fragment of childhood sitting at the edge of the world.

My father loved it.

Whenever he could, he'd bring my brother and me out here for burgers the size of our heads, chilli fries that could stop your heart, and milkshakes in more flavours than seemed possible. It became our ritual.

Despite the road around it slowly dying, the RAD had survived.

It had become something of a cult destination.

I was proudly one of its regular pilgrims.

Every visit felt like a quiet conversation with my father.

The owner, Bob Thorngood, had built the diner almost fifty years earlier. Nobody knew exactly what he'd done before that. Rumours ranged from mercenary work to treasure hunting, even espionage. Whatever the truth, it had left him with enough money—and enough grit—to build this chrome cathedral to mid-century Americana.

Bob was tough as leather.

And twice as weathered.

Years ago I'd written an article about the diner and its mythology. He loved it so much he had the entire piece laminated, framed and hung behind the counter like sacred scripture.

Ever since then he'd greeted me like a long-lost son.

As we pulled into one of the mostly empty parking bays, an unexpected calm settled over me.

We'd escaped the city.

We'd reached the edge of the Karee.

The edge of something vast...

and ancient.

More importantly—

we were beyond the Jackal's reach.

At least, I hoped we were.

If things went wrong again, Bob would have my back. He knew enough desert-hauliers who wouldn't think twice about introducing the Jackal's smug face to their fists.

Part of me had chosen this place for exactly that reason.

Winter had followed us out of Memphis, though it felt warmer inside the Mini than beneath the open sky. Outside, the desert air was sharp, dry and utterly unforgiving. It stole the moisture from your skin almost instantly. My lips cracked the moment I stepped out.

Sophie and I crossed the sun-bleached car park towards the wedge of shade beneath the diner's entrance canopy.

The RAD looked like a spaceship from a 1950s B-movie—all polished chrome and gleaming aluminium. Sunlight ricocheted from every curve, forcing us to squint whichever direction we looked.

Bright red and blue panels wrapped around the building, proudly refusing to belong to the modern world.

A vast curved window stretched across the front before sweeping around one side like the visor of some forgotten science-fiction robot.

Walking through the front door felt like stepping backwards through time.

The air conditioning greeted us first.

Cool.

Dry.

Then came the smell.

Grilled burgers.

Fryer oil.

Melted cheese.

Sweet syrup.

The RAD was immaculate.

Rows of oxblood-red leather booths gleamed beneath chrome fittings polished so often they reflected the lights like mirrors.

The whole place glowed with nostalgia.

Near the counter, an old jukebox pulsed softly, its coloured lights blinking to songs no one seemed to hear any more.

The diner had once been a true drive-in. Cars pulled alongside the building while roller-skating waitresses glided between them carrying towering trays of burgers and milkshakes.

That world had disappeared.

Bob simply refused to admit it.

Over the decades he'd transformed the diner into a museum of forgotten Americana.

Number plates.

Neon signs.

Petrol station clocks.

Model cars.

Film posters.

He displayed every piece with infectious pride.

Walking inside felt less like entering a restaurant than stepping into someone's happiest memories.

Business was quiet.

It usually was these days.

A handful of lorry drivers occupied the counter, swapping stories over endless mugs of coffee. Two bikers sat in a corner booth, their helmets resting beside them.

That was everyone.

Sophie and I slipped into a booth beside the window.

To one side, National Road 5 stretched back towards

Memphis, the city nothing more than a distant collection of towers shimmering on the horizon.

To the other...

only the endless, sun-bleached desert.

Before we'd even settled into our seats, a waitress appeared.

Young.

Pretty.

Bored.

She handed us menus without much enthusiasm.

We ordered quickly.

When she disappeared, silence returned.

Sophie leaned forward, staring into the vast emptiness beyond the glass.

Neither of us had spoken during the drive.

'So...'

I broke the silence.

'What are you thinking?'

She turned slowly.

Fear still lingered behind her eyes.

'Do you think he knows where we are?'

A pause.

'Will he come here?'

I considered the question before answering.

'I don't know.'

My stomach growled.

My head still throbbed from the beating.

'So...'

I hesitated.

'You believe me now?'

She looked away.

'I don't know what I believe, Abe.'

Pain flickered across her face.

She bit gently at her lower lip.

'He warned you not to come to me.'

She met my eyes again.

'Why didn't you listen?'

Her voice remained quiet.

'It would've saved both of us a lot of pain.'

'I know.'

I lowered my head.

'I'm sorry.'

The words felt painfully inadequate.

'It's just...'

I searched for something that could possibly explain it.

‘I knew you.’

‘I loved you.’

‘We loved each other.’

‘You asked me to find you.’

I looked up again.

‘I couldn’t walk away from that.’

I paused.

I needed her to understand.

‘Five years ago, I got shot.’

I paused.

‘Badly.’

‘I was in hospital for weeks. They weren’t sure I was going to make it.’

The memories still felt strangely close.

‘I was completely broken... and then it happened.’

I looked at her.

‘Right in the middle of all that pain, I had this moment of absolute clarity.’

I searched for words.

‘It was like a dam burst.’

‘A whole lifetime came flooding back.’

‘Your face.’

‘Your voice.’

'Us.'

She searched my expression, looking for something that would tell her whether I truly believed what I was saying.

'I never believed in any of this.'

I shook my head.

'I still don't know if I do—not in the way people usually mean it.'

A faint smile.

'But I couldn't unknow it.'

'I couldn't put those memories back where they came from.'

'They just... exploded into my mind.'

My smile faded.

'Out of everything I remembered... you were the strongest.'

'I remembered your promise.'

'I remembered mine.'

'I couldn't ignore that.'

Sophie sat very still.

Something was shifting behind her eyes.

'I know you don't remember.'

'I'm not asking you to accept everything without question.'

I hesitated.

'I just...'

My voice softened.

'I need you to give this a chance.'

A pause.

'Give us a chance.'

She didn't interrupt.

She simply listened.

'When I left hospital, I had no idea where to begin.'

I laughed quietly at the memory.

'So I bought a phone book.'

'Called hundreds of people pretending to be a journalist.'

'Nothing.'

'I divided the city into districts.'

'Went door to door.'

'Sat in cafés.'

'Walked shopping centres.'

'Talked to strangers.'

Another laugh.

'I think I've shaken hands with half of Memphis.'

A reluctant smile finally appeared on her face.

She slowly shook her head.

'I know how it sounds.'

'Obsessive.'

'Crazy.'

'Maybe it was.'

'I just couldn't stop.'

I looked down at my hands.

'Those memories felt like open wounds.'

'I believed you were the only person who could heal them.'

Something changed in her expression.

It landed.

'You never gave up.'

Her voice was almost a whisper.

'But how do you know it's really me?'

'I didn't.'

I smiled.

'Not at first.'

'I'd finally given up.'

'I accepted I'd failed.'

'Then you walked into that café.'

A warm memory crossed my face.

'I didn't consciously recognise you.'

'But some part of me did.'

She nodded slowly.

'I remember that.'

She smiled faintly.

'I thought you were a bit creepy.'

I laughed.

'Fair.'

'But...'

She frowned thoughtfully.

'I still sat down.'

'Something made me trust you.'

A playful smile appeared.

'You're kind of intense.'

'I know.'

We both laughed.

'When you left...'

I reached into my pocket.

'You dropped this.'

I unfolded the little chocolate wrapper.

The tiny knot remained perfectly tied.

Her eyebrows rose.

'I always do that.'

She laughed.

'Ever since I was little.'

'My parents used to tease me about it.'

I smiled.

'That's when I knew.'

I looked at the wrapper.

'And then the Jackal arrived.'

Her expression darkened.

'He confirmed it.'

'Exactly.'

I nodded.

'The moment he told me to stay away from you...'

'I stopped doubting.'

'Because he knew who you were too.'

She lowered her eyes.

'I still don't understand why he came after me.'

A long pause.

Then she looked back at me.

'But...'

She drew a slow breath.

'I believe you.'

Another pause.

'As impossible as all this sounds.'

Neither of us spoke.

'I'm sorry, Sophie.'

My voice was barely audible.

'For crashing into your life like this.'

'I know I've turned everything upside down.'

'I just hope...'

'I hope you can understand why I had to.'

The waitress arrived carrying our food and a fresh pot of coffee.

The interruption felt strangely ordinary.

I paid.

She disappeared.

Silence settled over the booth once more.

Sophie looked at me for what felt like forever.

Then she leaned across the table...

and kissed me.

The world exploded.

It wasn't simply a kiss.

Memory.

Emotion.

Recognition.

A lifetime compressed into a single heartbeat.

She pulled away slowly.

Her eyebrows lifted.

'This is insane.'

She laughed softly.

'You feel...'

She struggled for the words.

'You feel so right.'

She looked genuinely bewildered.

'How can someone I barely know feel this familiar?'

I smiled.

'Because you do know me.'

'You just don't remember me.'

She wrapped both hands around her coffee cup, letting the warmth soak into her fingers.

'I don't remember.'

A pause.

'And honestly...'

She looked away.

'That frightens me.'

'If you could remember,' I asked quietly, 'would you want to?'

She stared out across the desert for a long time.

'No.'

Her answer surprised me.

'Not unless I had to.'

She smiled sadly.

'I believe you.'

'That's enough.'

She drew a slow breath.

'But what if I remembered something I wished I'd forgotten?'

She looked back at me.

'For now...'

'I think it's okay if you carry those memories for both of us.'

A humourless laugh escaped her.

'Besides...'

'I still can't believe I hit the Jackal.'

She shook her head.

'I honestly thought I'd killed him.'

'Then he hit me back.'

She rubbed her jaw.

'I don't think people like him leave things unfinished.'

We both fell silent, remembering Gilbert Tower.

Eventually she smiled.

'Sorry about the kiss.'

I frowned.

'Why?'

'A friend once told me...'

She shrugged.

'If you kiss someone and see fireworks... don't walk away.'

I smiled.

But my thoughts lingered on something she'd said earlier.

She didn't want to remember.

Perhaps some part of her already did.

Perhaps the ending of our previous life still echoed somewhere inside her.

'Things didn't end well for us,' I said quietly.

'There was a war.'

'We lost each other far too soon.'

I looked at her.

'Maybe it's kinder that you don't remember.'

She reached across the table and gently took both my hands.

'Did I die?'

She hesitated.

'Did you?'

Almost immediately she shook her head.

'No.'

A small smile.

'Don't tell me.'

I nodded.

'Okay.'

Pain lingered behind her eyes.

I wished I'd never put it there.

'I just want you to know one thing.'

I squeezed her hands gently.

'I love you.'

'Whatever happens next...'

'I always will.'

Colour rose into her cheeks.

She didn't know how to answer.

Before she had the chance—

a shadow swept across our booth.

Both of us looked towards the car park.

A black car rolled silently into the space beside my old Mini.

Its windows were completely black.

Its polished body gleamed like obsidian beneath the desert sun.

My stomach tightened.

Something about it felt wrong.

Not merely dangerous...

wrong.

The engine continued idling.

Low.

Patient.

Like a predator deciding exactly when to strike.

Jupiter

Chapter six

Jupiter Invertida

Jupiter Reversed

Just then, Bob sauntered over with his usual faux-American swagger.

'Hey, Abe. Been a while. What's been keeping you?' He ruffled my hair like I was still a kid. 'I'm hoping she's the reason you've been neglecting us lately,' he added, flashing Sophie a knowing grin.

We both laughed nervously.

Our eyes kept drifting towards the black sedan idling beside my Mini.

Bob's smile faded.

'What?'

His gaze moved between us.

'You two look spooked.'

Then he looked properly at my face.

'Jesus... Abe.'

His expression hardened.

'What happened to you?'

'There's some psycho after us.'

My mouth felt dry.

'One of the bastards you warned me about.'

Everything about Bob changed.

The warmth vanished.

His shoulders squared.

The muscles in his jaw tightened.

It was like watching someone flick a switch.

'Who?'

His voice dropped.

'Where?'

He cracked his knuckles as his eyes swept across the car park.

'Who's giving you trouble, Abe?'

'I think he's in that black car.'

I swallowed.

'I'm going over to talk to him.'

'I just need you to cover me.'

Bob's jaw flexed.

'They did that to your face?'

'Yeah.'

'Stay here.'

He turned immediately.

'I'll be right back.'

As he disappeared inside, Sophie grabbed my hand.

'You can't go out there.'

Her voice shook.

'That lunatic nearly killed you already.'

'I know.'

I squeezed her hand.

'But Bob's got my back.'

I looked towards the sedan.

'If the Jackal tries anything... they'll deal with him.'

I tried to sound more confident than I felt.

'I just want to see if we can talk.'

My forehead was damp with sweat.

My stomach twisted like a knot of electric eels.

Moments later Bob returned.

Two enormous men walked beside him.

Their tattooed arms looked like tree trunks.

Neither bothered hiding the firearms beneath their jackets.

'These lads volunteered.'

Bob nodded towards them.

'If things kick off...'

He looked me squarely in the eye.

'Hit the deck and cover your head.'

'Got it.'

I finished my coffee in one swallow and stood.

Sophie tried to smile.

I managed something similar.

Then I headed outside.

The black sedan purred quietly beneath the winter sun.

I stopped for a moment before stepping off the porch.

The metallic taste of blood lingered in my mouth.

A few steps from the car, I glanced back.

Sophie stood behind the diner window with one hand pressed against the glass.

Something about that simple gesture steadied me.

It reminded me exactly why I was here.

Bob and his two companions stood several paces behind me.

Casual.

If you ignored the weapons.

I forced myself towards the driver's side window and knocked.

Then stepped back.

Nothing.

Several long seconds passed.

Finally—

the rear passenger window slid down with a soft mechanical hum.

Inside sat a balding man with carefully combed strands of hair stretched across his scalp.

He didn't even look up.

He simply continued writing.

Rectangular glasses slid repeatedly down his nose before he nudged them back into place with an impatient finger.

'Abe Mendes.'

His voice was quiet.

Cold.

'You've created rather an unfortunate situation.'

He continued writing.

'At approximately zero seven hundred hours this morning, your formal complaint was received.'

Another note.

'Shortly thereafter our assigned enforcement officer reported a deliberate breach of contract.'

Another note.

'You then allegedly assaulted said officer...'

He adjusted his glasses.

'Inflicted grievous bodily harm...'

Another note.

'...and threw him from a fifty-five-storey building.'

Only then did he finally glance up.

'Is that correct?'

The final words rose into an oddly bureaucratic question.

Before I could answer he continued.

'Subsequently...'

He consulted his notes.

‘You knowingly violated the completed terms of your agreement by re-establishing contact with the protected subject...’

He looked over the rim of his glasses.

‘Miss Sophie.’

Another note.

‘Furthermore...’

‘Said subject subsequently incapacitated our officer for a second time.’

He looked directly at me.

‘Making her a participating party in this dispute.’

A pause.

‘Is that also correct?’

The world suddenly felt absurd.

I kept expecting the Jackal to leap from somewhere nearby.

The desert wind whispered across the empty tarmac.

This man wasn’t the Jackal.

He was worse.

A bureaucrat.

I chose my words carefully.

‘I don’t think that’s a fair description of events.’

That finally got his attention.

He looked up.

His pudgy face twitched.

Then, without warning, he climbed out of the car.

He was much shorter than I'd imagined.

Immaculately dressed.

Shoes polished to a mirror shine.

'Not fair?'

His voice sharpened.

He marched right up to me.

I had to lower my head just to meet his eyes.

'Please...'

He hissed.

'Enlighten me.'

'Tell me the fair version.'

Heat rolled off him.

Barely controlled.

'Your agent's a psychopath,' I said evenly.

'Everything I did was self-defence.'

His face turned crimson.

Then darker still.

'I also dispute the agreement.'

I folded my arms.

‘I don’t remember consenting to any of it.’

He froze.

His lips trembled.

Then—

‘YOU!’

He stamped one polished shoe into the dust.

‘YOU!’

Another stamp.

Dust exploded around him.

‘YOU!’

His face became almost purple.

Finally—

‘FUCK!’

He spun around, slammed the car door, and the window shot shut.

Silence.

Only the wind remained.

I looked back towards the diner.

Sophie stared at me through the glass, completely bewildered.

Behind her, Bob and the others watched with expressions somewhere between concern and amusement.

I shrugged helplessly.

Sophie slapped a hand across her forehead.

I turned back and knocked again.

'Excuse me?'

Nothing.

'We'd really like to resolve this.'

Still nothing.

'It's been a very long day.'

I sighed.

'We'd quite like to go home.'

After a few seconds the rear door opened.

This time a woman stepped gracefully onto the tarmac.

Bright orange hair.

A perfectly tailored grey suit.

Long crimson fingernails like polished talons.

Her smile was immaculate.

'You've upset the Under-Secretary-General of Reports and Communications.'

She smiled pleasantly.

'He's asked me to intervene.'

She approached with measured confidence.

'Firstly...'

She clasped her hands.

'Only accredited negotiators may renegotiate existing contracts.'

‘Since you failed to appoint suitable representation...’

She smiled sweetly.

‘You’ll need to obtain some.’

‘Quickly.’

She sniffed delicately.

‘Otherwise another representative will be appointed on your behalf.’

A tiny smile.

‘Which, if memory serves...’

‘...is exactly how this unfortunate situation began.’

She stepped closer.

‘Last time you waived your right to independent representation.’

Her smile widened.

‘Now you’re dissatisfied with the outcome.’

She sighed.

‘Typical.’

She leaned towards me.

Her voice became razor sharp.

‘Do you currently have appropriate representation?’

Only then did I notice her teeth.

Perfect.

White.

Far too pointed to be human.

'I...'

I swallowed.

'How long have I got?'

Her smile disappeared.

'No extension.'

'Twenty-four hours.'

'Fail to secure representation...'

She tilted her head.

'...and your rights will be forfeited.'

'You'll be recycled.'

A pause.

'Destination determined without consultation.'

Another smile.

'As for the young lady...'

She glanced towards Sophie.

'Her memories will be removed.'

She slowly licked her lips.

Then—

an engine roared across the desert.

A motorcycle screamed off the highway.

Too fast.

Far too fast.

The Jackal.

He skidded sideways behind the sedan in a shower of sparks before throwing himself from the bike.

Fury poured off him.

'There you are, you little shit!'

He pointed straight at me.

'Wait till I get my hands on you and your bitch!'

'I'll make you beg!'

'Jay!'

The orange-haired woman snapped.

With surprising ease she shoved him backwards.

'Calm yourself.'

'A complaint has been lodged.'

'You've lost jurisdiction.'

'Until the dispute is resolved...'

She pointed at Sophie and me.

'They're off limits.'

She smiled.

'If they fail...'

'Then they're yours again.'

The Jackal groaned.

'Aw... bollocks.'

Behind me the diner door swung open.

Bob emerged.

The two mountain-sized men followed.

One carried a tyre iron.

The other...

a sawn-off shotgun.

'This bloke bothering you, Abe?'

Bob called.

He wasn't joking.

The Jackal snarled.

The orange-haired woman slapped him sharply across the face.

Then she turned towards Bob with flawless manners.

'No trouble at all.'

She smiled.

'Simply delivering an administrative message.'

She looked back at me.

'Isn't that right, sweetie?'

She winked.

Then slipped elegantly back into the sedan.

The Jackal climbed reluctantly onto his motorcycle.

He glared at me.

Slowly licked his lips.

Then disappeared in a roar of engines.

The sedan drifted silently after him.

Only when they vanished beyond the highway did I finally breathe.

Then I remembered Madame Bea's card.

I pulled it from my pocket.

Black.

Glossy.

Embossed with the image of a strange figure—half man,

half goat—seated alone in a field.

There was only one path left.

I had to find the Devil.

He was the only negotiator I had left.

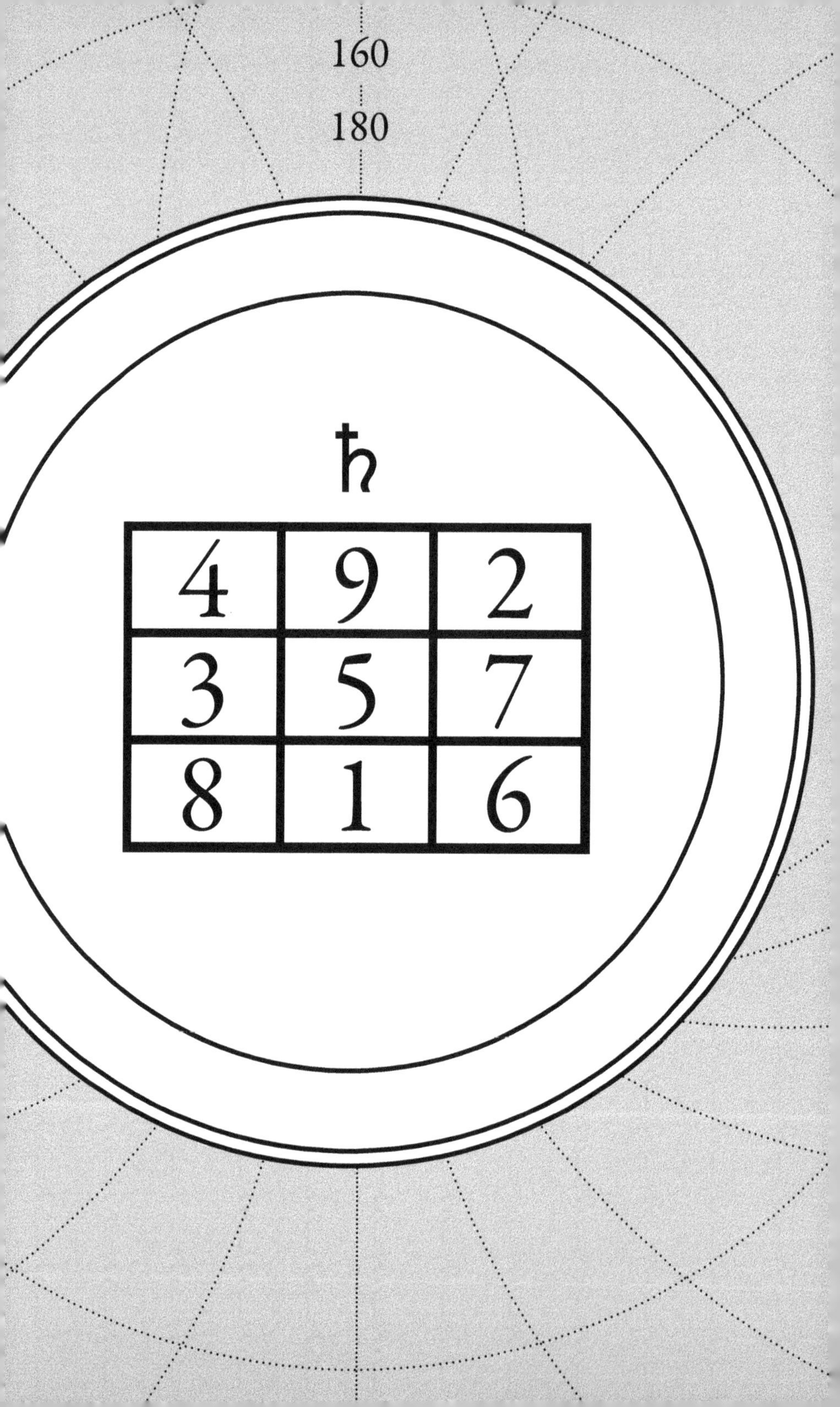
160
180
♄
4 9 2
3 5 7
8 1 6

Part three

WINGS OF STATIC

The pulse between collapse and flight — motion learning its shape.

He approaches.

Their antennae touch.

The air breaks open.

The dance begins—

circling,

colliding,

surrendering.

A geometry of hunger.

When they join, it is both devotion and violence.

Wings tremble.

Shells grind.

The sound is like prayer swallowed by flame.

The Star

Chapter one

A estrela novamente

The Star Again

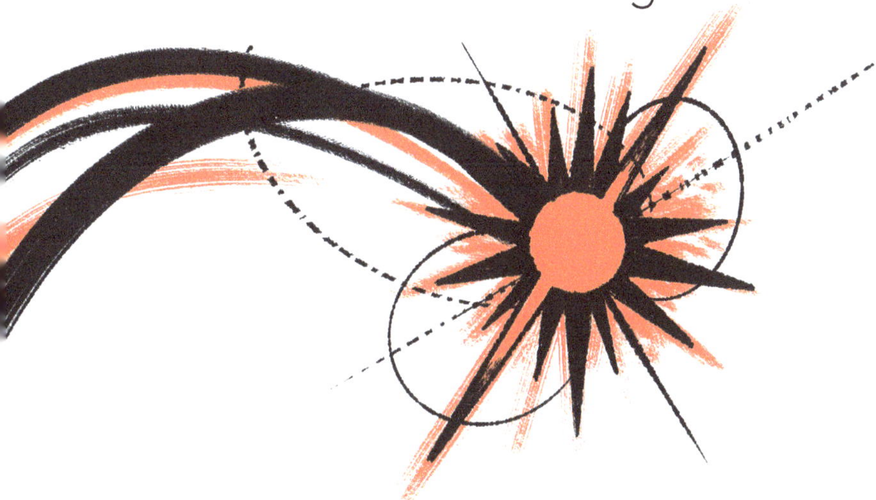

'What kind of mess are you in, Abe?' Bob asked as I walked back towards the door. 'I've seen my fair share of weirdos pass through here, but those three were next-level crazy.'

He wasn't wrong. They were the strangest people I'd ever encountered. I didn't even try to defend them.

'Thanks, Bob,' I said. 'For everything.'

The two giants who'd flanked him earlier lumbered off into the shadowy interior of the RAD, disappointed there hadn't been a fight. Bob lingered, his eyes searching my face, trying to find an explanation that would somehow make sense of the surreal freak show he had just witnessed.

I gave him a lie. A safe one, carefully crafted to fit comfortably within his view of the world.

'I've been working on a story. Investigating organised crime families out in Memphis.'

He seemed to accept it, but the look in his eyes told me he didn't believe the whole story. Bob wasn't dim. He could smell a half-truth a mile away.

'Well, I'm glad I could help, Abe,' he said, lowering his voice. 'But when you leave here, keep your wits about you. Those people aren't just crazy—they're padded-room, heavy-medication crazy. You understand me?'

I gave a weak laugh, even though it wasn't funny.

It was worse than crazy.

The desert wind had picked up, dry and biting, kicking sand into swirling clouds. The sun was beginning to dip, casting long shadows across the empty land. I made my way back to our booth, my skin cold and my thoughts colder.

Sophie stood as I approached and wrapped her arms around me.

I sank into her.

Her embrace was a harbour—safe, warm, untouched by madness.

I closed my eyes and breathed her in, letting myself disappear for a moment.

We held each other for a long time, oblivious to everything beyond us. The kind of embrace you hope will last forever.

But it never does.

'What happened?' she whispered at last, her head resting against my shoulder.

I told her everything.

By the time I finished, we were seated again. Her eyes had grown distant and glassy. There was too much to take in. Too many impossible things had already happened.

And I still hadn't told her the worst part.

'I have a card,' I said carefully. 'Someone who might be able to help renegotiate the deal.'

Her expression changed immediately.

'Wait... what? You know someone? A valid representative? How? Are you going to call them? Are they even human?'

I answered her last question first.

'No,' I said. 'He's one of them.'

I touched my face. The swelling was beginning to go down.

'There's no number to call. He doesn't do phones. He

lives out there.' I pointed beyond the roadside towards the endless desert. 'I've got rough directions.'

Sophie followed my hand. The landscape beyond the glass was barren, wind-scoured and endless. The horizon stretched in a perfectly straight line, as though reality itself had been drawn with a ruler.

'You know anyone else?' she asked, hope flickering briefly before fading again.

'No.' I poured us both another coffee. 'He's the only one.'

She leaned forward slightly, sensing the change in my voice. I braced myself.

'The card belongs to someone called El Diablo.'

I slid it across the table.

She picked it up cautiously. Her eyebrows lifted.

Then her mouth slowly fell open.

'Yeah,' I said. 'That Devil. But apparently not the one we think. I've been told it's... not quite that simple.'

Her hands trembled almost imperceptibly as she turned the card over beneath the light.

'What other choice do we have?' I asked quietly.

'I'm sorry, Sophie. I never meant for you to get caught up in all this.'

She looked at me for a long moment before speaking.

'I'm starting to think... I wouldn't have wanted it any

other way.'

I blinked in surprise.

She caught my expression and smiled gently.

'There's a whole other world running alongside ours,' she said softly. 'And I never even knew it existed until you showed me. That alone changes everything. But also... there's you and me. We're connected, Abe. It took me a while to realise it, but I believe you now.'

She reached across the table, took my hands in hers, and held my gaze without flinching.

'Thank you for finding me.

Thank you for keeping your promise.'

My chest tightened.

My eyes welled up again.

We were two fools sitting at the edge of the world, with a ticking clock and one impossible chance left.

But we were together.

She smiled.

I laughed.

Beyond the great wraparound windows, the Karee Desert waited in silent anticipation.

The Hermit

Chapter two

O Eremita

The Hermit

‘They all mention the same thing,’ she continued.

‘The Black House.’

I turned towards her.

‘What, like a ghost story?’

‘Sort of.’ She laughed softly at herself. ‘But it isn’t just one story. It’s more like... a pattern. Something people keep seeing. Drivers say that when you’ve been out there too long, and your mind starts wandering, you sometimes catch sight of something that shouldn’t exist.’

Now she had my full attention.

‘They say a blackened house, scorched as though it had

burned to the ground, simply appears. Standing alone beside the road, shimmering in the heat haze. Some people think it's a mirage. Others say it's a warning. But they all agree on one thing.'

She looked back towards the desert.

'The Karee changes people. It's almost as if it listens... then decides what it wants to show you.'

I followed her gaze.

The emptiness suddenly felt far less empty.

'This place has always felt different to me,' I said quietly. 'Ever since my dad brought me here as a kid. There's something ancient beneath the sand. Something watching.'

I paused.

'And I don't know, Sophie... I think I do have the faith. I think something out there is waiting to find me.'

The wind filled the silence between us.

'I'm coming with you.'

There wasn't even a hint of hesitation.

'I was thinking... maybe you shouldn't.'

I turned towards her.

'Maybe it's better if you stay. If something happens to me, maybe they'll leave you alone. Maybe they'll wipe your memory and let you go.'

Her eyes flashed.

She stamped her boot into the hard earth.

'Don't you dare try to leave me behind again, Abe.'

Her voice cracked like a whip.

'If these are going to be our last hours, then I'm spending them with you.'

For a moment I couldn't answer.

I wanted her beside me.

I was terrified of what that might cost her.

'You're right,' I said at last, my voice barely above a whisper. 'It was a stupid idea.'

She reached for my hand and held it tightly.

'Then let's go.'

She looked towards the endless horizon.

'Let's find him. Whoever... whatever... he is.'

The desert offered no promises.

No guarantees.

Only the unknown.

Together, we stepped forward.

The Sun

Chapter three

O Sol

The Sun

The car jerked onto the highway, hesitating as though it knew better. As if it, too, feared the vast nothing that stretched out between cities—between realities. The petrol gauge hovered near empty—exactly as I'd intended. We would drive until we ran out of fuel, then wait. That was what Madame Bea said would summon him. The Prince. The one who would find us if we needed help.

It felt absurd.

But also, strangely right.

The road stretched out before us like a black ribbon through bone-dry silence. Sophie and I joked nervously to break the tension—taking jabs at the Jackal and his bosses, laughing too hard just to keep fear from creeping in. At some point, the conversation quietened, and we turned to look at the scorched wilderness rolling past our windows.

I had fallen in love with the desert a long time ago.

There's something about it—something ancient. It holds secrets buried in silence. The desert doesn't distract.

It confronts.

Out here, there's nothing to look at but the raw landscape and, eventually, yourself. It's a mirror that reflects your soul back at you—mercilessly.

Some people can't handle it. They grow restless, disturbed. The silence presses too hard, the emptiness too vast. But others see beauty in it. Mystery. They recognise the shadows and welcome them.

The desert doesn't change.

It reveals.

It peels back the layers we've spent our whole lives building until only something true remains.

There's no coming back from the desert unchanged.

Sophie and I both felt it—its strange gravity pulling us inward. We were on the threshold of something irreversible. Something sacred.

Up ahead, the highway shimmered in the heat, and a long line of cars and caravans came into view. Some had pulled off the tarmac entirely, scattered across the sand in small, chaotic clusters. Music drifted through the air, heavy with bass, a living pulse that thudded against the emptiness. Figures danced on van roofs and along the roadside, their bodies wrapped in flowing fabrics and bursts of colour that seemed almost unreal against the pale desert backdrop.

'What is this?' Sophie leaned forward, eyes wide.

'The festival,' I said, slowing the car a little. 'They drive out from Memphis every year. Artists, dreamers, runaways—whoever wants to disappear for a while. I wrote about it once for Pulse, but I never thought I'd actually see it.'

As we passed, a woman in mirrored sunglasses waved lazily, and a shirtless man spun fire on the roof of a caravan. Sophie watched in silence, her face lit by the strange glow of it all—the laughter, the movement, the fleeting sense of freedom.

'Looks... beautiful,' she murmured.

'It is,' I said. 'And it only gets more so when night falls—the lights, the fire, the stars. It's as if the desert keeps the music alive after dark.'

I pressed the accelerator, and the sound of the music began to fade, swallowed by the engine's hum, before the desert swallowed it whole.

I stuck the Devil's business card to the windscreen.

Sophie kicked her boots up onto the dashboard. It was too cold to roll the windows down, or we would have let the wind tangle our hair and pretended we were kids again—on some enchanted family road trip, back when magic still felt possible.

The sun was past its zenith, hanging low in a sea of pure blue. Two in the afternoon. Fifteen hours left. The horizon was a wasteland of flatness and fractured rock—jagged, alien, like debris from a broken planet. The rocks looked misplaced, random, as though they'd fallen from space. There was a pattern in their chaos, but it refused to be read.

We talked to keep the silence at bay. We spoke of childhood, old schools, favourite hiding spots, and the small joys that had built our lives. It was effortless, as though the past had never left us. Memories of another life—our real life—wove themselves into our stories. And despite the danger, the strangeness, the looming unknown, I had never felt happier.

'What's that?' Sophie shouted, pointing beyond the windscreen.

I flinched at the sudden sound, swerving slightly.

'Jesus! You scared the hell out of me,' I said, scanning

the road. 'Thought we hit something.'

Then I saw it. Relief washed through me.

'Oh—that? That's The Pimple.'

'The Pimple?' she echoed, laughing.

'My mum's name for it. It's the only thing out here that sticks out.'

A mesa rose ahead of us—red and black stone towering above the flat horizon. Its top was wide and flat, like a table. The sides were steep, almost vertical in places. It looked ancient. Majestic. Silent. The butte loomed larger as we neared, dominating the desert around it.

'I think it's a mesa. Or a butte. My dad told me once, but I only remember Pimple.' I laughed.

'Can we stop?' she asked, pressing her forehead against the dashboard, trying to look up at the summit.

'Sure.'

I pulled off the road, slowing beside its eastern slope. We rolled to a halt in its short, cold shadow.

Sophie leapt out before I had even killed the engine. She gazed upward, eyes wide with childlike awe.

'This is amazing! Why didn't I know about this place?'

I followed her to the base. It was colder here, the shadow biting through my jacket.

'Wouldn't it be something to sit at the top,' I said, teeth chattering, 'just watching the world in its silent glory...

with a thermos of soup or something?'

She looked over her shoulder, her eyes glowing with that light I remembered—like she could make the world feel brand new.

'Let's go, then!' she laughed—and took off up the slope.

I blinked, stunned—but she was already halfway up. I had no choice but to follow. This butte had lived in my imagination since childhood. I used to beg my parents to stop when we drove past, always wanting to climb it. They never did.

Now, here I was—chasing Sophie up its sandy flank, heart pounding with the joy of old dreams reborn.

We climbed hard for twenty minutes, the slope steep and relentless. At last, we reached the sheer cliff wall at the top, leaning against its stone surface and catching our breath. It was easy to imagine slipping and falling all the way back down.

'There has to be a way up,' Sophie said between breaths. She moved carefully along the rock face, tracing its curve. Then we stepped back into sunlight, and the warmth hit our skin like a drug.

There—nestled in a fold of the rock—was a rough path winding upward. We didn't know if it had been carved by hands or worn by time, but it was climbable. We scrambled up, finding footholds and handholds, pulling ourselves to the summit.

And then—

we were there.

The world stretched away in every direction. A tapestry of browns and greys, of patterns visible only from this height. The sky arched above us like an unbroken dome from one horizon to the next.

I ran to her, swept her off her feet and spun her around until we both collapsed into the dust, laughing, dizzy, breathless, alive.

We kissed—electric, endless—and then sat side by side, watching the desert stretch out beneath us.

'I never imagined I'd end up here when I woke up this morning,' Sophie said, her voice tinged with wonder. 'Whatever happens, Abe… thank you.'

A single tear traced her cheek.

'I was angry at first, for showing up and wrecking my life. But now? This is something people wait a lifetime for.'

She turned to the horizon.

'Just… going. Letting the current carry us wherever it wants. I don't know where we'll end up, but I hope it's with you.'

I kissed her again, overwhelmed.

That moment made everything worth it. The fear. The Jackal. The unknown. I would have walked to the end of the Earth for those words.

We'd lost an hour climbing, but gained something

eternal. It was nearly half three now. The sun still had hours to burn.

'This is how we used to be, Sophie.

I let the words settle between us.

'This is how we're meant to be.'

I breathed in deeply. The air felt crisp. Pure. Like it had never been breathed before.

'Tell me, Abey,' she said softly. 'Tell me about us. Who I was. Who we were.'

She looked into me. Past the moment. Into something timeless.

I spoke until the afternoon drifted quietly around us, telling her about our little corner of the old city. About our neighbourhood. Our stolen glances in school corridors. The warmth of first love. The heartbreak. The reunion. The city. Our quiet little home.

I stopped short before the fall.

She cradled my face in her palms, pulling me close, kissing me with an aching tenderness.

The words escaped before I could stop them.

'Marry me.'

'In this and every lifetime,' she said, and smiled.

The Prince

Chapter four

O Príncipe

The Prince

The descent was ten times worse than the climb. Every second step felt like the beginning of a fall that might never end. More than once, I pictured myself cartwheeling down the slope, a rag doll flung by gravity. Somehow, we made it. Back to the Mini. Back to shelter. Giddy with relief and half-frozen, we tumbled inside, breathless and hysterical. Our laughter was high-pitched and wild—part joy, part madness from the cold. Our muscles ached, already stiffening from the brutal climb. The ascent had been spontaneous, beautiful, reckless. But what had happened at the top would stay with me forever, branded into my heart like a sacred mark. I didn't need sore legs to remember.

With a screech of tyres and a jolt of engine, I yanked us back onto the road. Our self-sabotaging mission resumed: drive until the fuel ran dry, then wait for the Prince.

The butte—the Pimple—shrank in the rear-view mirror, a vanishing monument behind us. By the time the engine stuttered and coughed its last breath, it was just after 4:45. The Mini groaned, juddered, then rolled to a dead stop at the shoulder of the highway. The wind had picked up, furious and freezing, dragging howls across the barren flats. Dust devils erupted around the car like desert phantoms. I stepped out into the chaos.

Sand struck me like shrapnel, blinding and bitter. It scraped at my eyes and filled my mouth. Above us, the sky was still a pristine, unshaken blue—but around us? A roiling storm of earth and wind. I had to shout for Sophie to hear me. She joined me outside, her hair already whipped into a frenzy.

I moved to where she stood, cupping my hands around my mouth to yell.

'Well! This is it!' I roared above the gale. My legs felt heavy and numb. Her face was flushed red from the cold, her nose running, lips a ghostly blue—but she still smiled.

'This is insane!' she hollered.

It was. Completely. We had staked everything on a mad

set of instructions and a stranger I didn't even know by name. But standing beside her, even the madness made sense. I turned from her, faced the wind, and screamed. Not words—just a primal roar. I swung my arms wide like a prophet on the edge of revelation.

Whether by coincidence or something stranger, the wind suddenly died, as though my defiance had carried power. The dust fell like a curtain, revealing the world again—stark and dry, the highway stretching endlessly in both directions. The sun dipped lower, brushing the horizon with slow inevitability.

'Ha!' I shouted in mock triumph, arms raised.

Sophie burst out laughing at the absurd timing. She climbed onto the Mini's bonnet and folded into a lotus pose, exhaling.

'So, this Prince,' she said, grinning. 'Is he even human? And how's he supposed to know we're here?'

I joined her on the bonnet. 'I have no idea. I don't even know his name. Arabian prince? Knight of the Round Table? Lancelot or Aladdin?'

'Mmm... horse or flying carpet?' she teased.

A stillness had settled. An unnatural quiet. We fell into it, as though the desert had hushed to hear what came next.

'Wait,' I said, holding up a hand. I tilted my head, straining. There—it was faint, but growing louder. A low rumble on the wind.

'You hear that?' I asked.

She did—her eyes were closed, one ear cupped to the air like a tuning fork. We both slid off the bonnet, adrenaline surging. A shadow emerged on the northern stretch of road. Something big. Fast. A truck.

As it closed the distance, details sharpened. It was definitely a tow truck—patched together from mismatched panels, painted in a mosaic of rust and salvage-yard colours. It barrelled toward us like a missile. For a second, I thought it wouldn't stop.

But fifty metres out, the driver slammed the brakes.

The truck shrieked, tyres smoking, skidding sideways before finally lurching to a halt right beside us. The air reeked of scorched rubber and petrol. I hacked and coughed, swatting away the smog.

Painted across the side of the truck in elegant, looping white script were the words:

Prince's Tow and Panelbeater Services.

The truck coughed, spluttered, and died with a groan. A moment later, the passenger door snapped open.

Through the open door, we saw him: a thin, wiry man sitting behind the wheel, his skin dark as mahogany, the whites of his eyes sharp and startling against the shadowed interior of the cab. He looked from me to Sophie, then back again. And then he smiled—a wide, gleaming grin that radiated warmth. Suspicion drained out of me. There was something unmistakably good about this man. Prince was, without a doubt, a good egg.

'Hai!' he called, waving.

'Hello,' I replied, stepping cautiously closer.

'Are you... the Prince?' I asked, awkward and uncertain.

'Yes! I'm Prince. That's my name,' he said proudly, pointing to his chest.

'Oh,' I laughed, catching the misunderstanding. 'Right. I need help. Can you take me to El Diablo?'

He didn't flinch. Didn't ask questions. Just smiled and hopped out of the cab. His outfit was as eccentric as his truck—stone-washed jeans, a black T-shirt with 'Prince' screen-printed across it in light purple, and grey trainers laced with luminous green strings. His energy was infectious, bouncing around us as if we were old friends.

'What's the trouble?' he asked, circling the Mini without waiting for an answer to my question about the Devil. 'You hit a coyote? Crash into—' He stopped, probably realising there was nothing out here to crash into.

'Ran out of fuel,' I said.

Prince let out a long whistle and surveyed the empty highway, squinting like he was trying to summon a memory.

'No kidding, man. You're in trouble. No petrol stations for miles.' He paused, then shrugged. 'But I'm a panelbeater.'

We must have looked confused because he quickly explained. 'I fix cars. If they crash, I bend them back. Cut out the busted bits, weld in new ones—scavenged parts mostly. Beat 'em straight, paint 'em up. Good as new.'

I nodded. Prince was like a back-alley surgeon for broken-down cars. His accent was faint but difficult to place—perhaps southern African, with a rhythm in his words that suggested a life far from here.

'This truck,' he said proudly, patting the side. 'She's my project. You should've seen her before—straight from the dump. She's coming along nicely. Just needs a few more pieces. Then she'll be beautiful.'

He busied himself at the rear of the truck, fiddling with chains and hooks. Then, without warning, he leapt back into the cab. The engine roared to life again, the truck jerking forward in a spasm. He spun the wheel in an extreme arc and charged twenty metres ahead before the engine cut again. Sophie and I stood frozen, wide-eyed.

I glanced at Sophie. We were thinking exactly the same thing.

This guy's taking us to the Devil? Seriously?

The truck's reverse lights flared, and it backed up smoothly until the rear hovered just over the Mini. Prince leapt out and got to work with the chains, humming and chuckling to himself.

'You'll take us to see the Devil?' I asked again.

Prince kept working, not answering. His hands moved quickly, threading chains beneath the Mini.

'Your lady will have to sit in the car,' he said without looking up. 'You'll ride up front with me.' He pointed a bony finger at me.

'Uh...' I hesitated.

'No room for both of you. And I'll need your help.'

'Is she safe back there?' I asked.

'Safe, safe,' he said impatiently, still working the levers. The Mini lifted slightly off the ground.

Sophie looked uneasy.

'I don't know if it's safe to ride in a towed car...'

It didn't feel right to me either. But Prince was adamant, hopping in and out of the Mini's passenger seat to prove his point.

'You see? You see?' he repeated.

Eventually, Sophie relented. I helped her into the front seat of the Mini, which now sat just a foot off the ground. She leaned back, stretched her legs across the seat, and tried to look relaxed.

'I might just nap back here,' she joked, but I saw the nervousness in her eyes.

Prince and I walked to the front of the truck. As I climbed into the passenger seat, a wave of petrol fumes hit me like a punch to the throat.

'What's that smell?' I asked, covering my nose.

In the middle of the seat sat a plastic bucket filled with a copper-coloured liquid, sloshing ominously.

'That? Petrol.' Prince shrugged. 'Still haven't found a proper tank.' A hosepipe snaked out of the bucket, disappearing beneath the dashboard, rigged together with wire and a soaked rag that did nothing to stop the drip... drip... drip... of fuel.

'I found a carburettor last week!' he added proudly. 'Here—hold this for me.'

He passed me the bucket.

I accepted it as though he'd handed me a live grenade.

'Is it dangerous?' I asked.

'No, no, no.' He laughed it off, but even he didn't sound convinced. Dangerous or not, we had no other option. I cradled the bucket and tried to ignore the sting of the fumes.

'Please keep the hose in the petrol,' he said gently as he turned the key.

The truck shook violently and refused to start.

'Ahh... new carburettor. She's stubborn.'

He fiddled, pumped the pedal, muttered something under his breath, then suddenly the engine roared to life like an angry animal.

Prince whooped and punched the air.

We tore down the highway with my Mini dancing alarmingly behind us.

The sun had sunk lower, but we still had some light left. I turned to check on Sophie. She smiled and waved. I waved back, but Prince scolded me for letting go of the bucket.

The wind tore through the open windows. My fingers were turning blue, but Prince looked completely unfazed.

'Where are we going?' I asked.

Prince gave me a strange look, like I'd asked if water was wet.

'You asked me to take you to him.'

'You fix cars and take people to the Devil?'

'Yes, that was the deal.' He glanced at me. 'I came here, long time ago. From South Africa. But first, we lived in Botswana. You been there?'

I shook my head.

'No, neither.'

'One day we go!' he laughed. His joy was infectious. Even under the weight of petrol fumes, I smiled.

'I'll show you around. Beautiful place.'

He looked away then, lost in something wistful. I knew he didn't mean it. We wouldn't go anywhere together.

Still, I smiled back.

I couldn't figure him out. Prince, this oddball panelbeater in the middle of nowhere, casually connected to the Devil. It didn't make sense, and a thousand questions burned inside me.

'My father brought us here when I was a kid,' he said suddenly, unprompted. 'I went back once. Met my cousins again. The friends I used to play with. They tried to teach me Tswana.'

'Will you go back?' I asked.

He laughed.

'Maybe—when my contract's up.'

He reached into the glove box and pulled out a battered pack of cigarettes, flicking one into his mouth. Then he offered me one.

'You're going to smoke? Next to this?' I shifted uneasily, nudging the open bucket of petrol on my lap away from him.

'Nah. It's okay. Really. Smoking's okay.'

He waved dismissively, like he hadn't just lit a match within inches of a bomb.

As the acrid smoke mingled with the choking petrol fumes, Prince puffed happily, launching into a story about his life back home—his friends, his father, and the tangle of wives that filled his childhood. The truck slowed and veered gently off the highway, tyres crunching over a sandy embankment. A narrow dirt road branched off from the tarmac, disappearing into the arid wilderness. Prince eased the truck onto it, glancing back to make sure my Mini was still tracking behind.

The petrol in the bucket sloshed dangerously close to the rim, but I kept it balanced.

'All good!' Prince chirped, returning his focus to the wheel.

I kept quiet, gazing out the window. The desert had begun to change around us. Low brush crept in, tough grey-green shrubs reaching their thorny fingers across the sand. We'd been rattling along the dirt track for nearly half an hour when shapes started forming on the horizon—hills rising from the flat expanse ahead.

'He lives out here,' Prince said. 'Crowds bother him now. But people still come. They want something. Looking to strike a deal. Only I know the way. Don't worry—I'll take you.'

A pause settled between us before I asked the question that had been gnawing at me.

'Is he really the Devil?'

Prince glanced sideways, his grin curling slowly.

'Who's the Devil?' he asked. 'He was alive long before the Devil you've heard about was even invented. Then somebody got clever. Figured they could scare people into behaving by making him the villain. They lumped in all the things they didn't want people doing and slapped his name on it. Poof. Now he's the Devil.'

'So... he's not?'

'The Devil with horns and cloven hooves?' Prince scoffed. 'That's just a bedtime story some people weaponised. Control through fear. Love their god by hating this guy. Clever trick.'

'He's not pure evil, if that's what you mean. But he's real. Not a fallen angel or some televangelist scapegoat. They just saw what he looked like—different—and decided that made him dangerous.'

They rewrote him.

That broke something in him.

The sun had dropped lower still. The dirt road twisted toward the base of the hills, skirting their edges. The terrain had changed completely. Towering cacti rose like green sentinels from the dry earth, crowding around boulders and brambles. As we neared the foothills, they grew denser, forming something like a forest.

'His heart broke, so he withdrew. Hid himself away. Now he only helps those willing to go far enough to find him,' Prince said with a strange pride. 'Now he wears the title like a badge. Lemons into lemonade, right?'

We began descending into a narrow gully, dropping into a wide, shallow basin. Nestled at the bottom, invisible from the flat desert above, was a structure—dark and unwelcoming.

It was a house.

Black.

Waiting.

Black as coal. A double-storey Victorian house, perhaps Edwardian, with a covered porch stretching across the front. The timber looked charred, and even the window frames had been painted black. Everything about it exhaled secrecy. My heart thudded in my throat.

Prince stopped the truck about twenty metres away. The surrounding ground was barren—no cacti, no rocks, no brush. Just emptiness and the house.

'Well,' Prince said, his tone suddenly grave, 'here you are.'

He reached for the bucket. I passed it over carefully, my trousers damp with sweat and petrol. Once outside, I hurried around the truck to check on Sophie. She was already out of the Mini, standing still, staring at the black house. It creaked in the wind, as if groaning beneath the weight of its own silence. She turned to me and offered an uncertain smile.

'Well, we made it before sundown,' I said.

Eleven hours remained.

Somehow, we were ahead of schedule.

'How was the ride?' I asked.

'Amazing,' she said, eyes gleaming. 'I thought it'd be rough, but it was like… floating. Like we were gliding across the sand on air.'

I smiled, even as my nerves pulled tight.

'Well,' she said brightly, grabbing my hand, 'let's go meet the Devil!'

'You can't,' Prince said from behind us.

We both turned.

'Only he can.' Prince pointed at me, his expression grave. He looked older suddenly, weathered by something invisible.

'The Devil only sees one person at a time. Visiting hours are from sunrise to sundown—so if you want your chance, you'd better get moving.'

The sky had deepened into a burnished orange. The sun was skimming the rim of the Earth. I swallowed, uneasy. I didn't like leaving Sophie behind.

'But what I need to say… it involves her too,' I said.

'No matter,' Prince replied, his voice firmer now. 'You can make more than one deal—if the terms are fair. But he won't see you both at once.'

As he finished speaking, something shifted.

Prince looked older.

Much older.

His skin had gone thin and wrinkled, his hair white

as bone. A wooden cane was suddenly in his hand. Slowly, he hobbled towards the porch.

A rocking chair waited there, next to a small table. On it sat a tall glass of

water, a slice of lemon hooked over the rim.

Prince climbed the steps, creaking with every footfall, and settled into the chair.

He leaned his cane against the table, pulled out a pipe, and lit it. The chair rocked gently beneath him as he puffed on the pipe, eyes far away, already somewhere else.

In less than a minute, he had become an old man.

Sophie and I stood at the edge of the strange black house and watched the last light fade from the sky.

The HangingMan

Chapter five

O Homem Enforcado Invertida

The Hanging Man Reversed

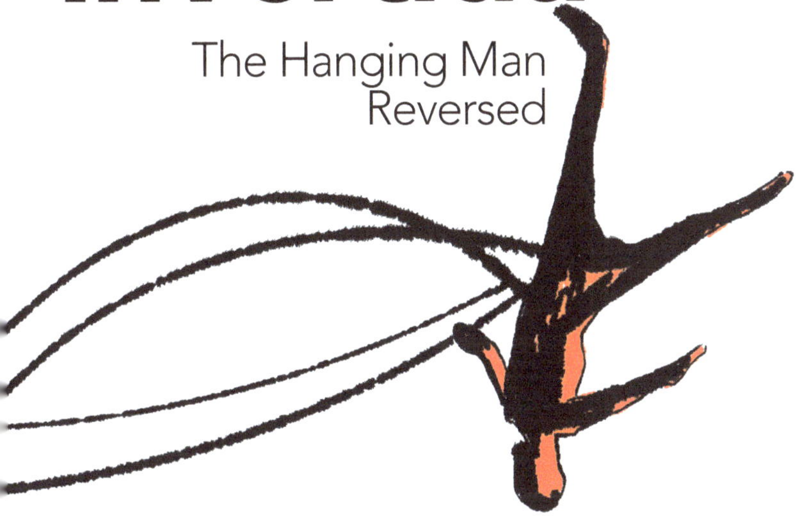

We were barely three metres from the veranda before the blackened walls of the house loomed above us. The front door was fitted with a silver handle that glinted with the last sliver of winter light, catching the dying sun like a flame. The house wasn't dilapidated or crude—it was immaculately crafted. Carved wooden posts, detailed with flowing, sculptural motifs, lined the ornate façade. Beauty, however, didn't soften the unease it provoked. There was something wrong with the place—something that gnawed quietly at the edges of my mind.

Sophie stepped up to the veranda, her eyes wide, her fingers tracing the intricate carvings on the stairs and railing.

'Wow. Abe, look at this,' she whispered, enchanted.

'Yes,' Prince said from the rocking chair, his voice distant. 'He carved every inch of it once. Used to be a carpenter... before he became something else.'

The house groaned softly. That creaking sound—it stirred a half-buried memory, nudging the suspicion already curling in my gut. I moved toward the left side of the veranda, guided by instinct, pulled to the far front corner of the house.

The unease bloomed into something sharper. My movements became automatic. I needed to prove my suspicion wrong—needed to walk the perimeter and see the house for what it was.

I rounded the corner—and shouted. The truth hit me in the chest.

There was no black house.

It was a lie. A shell. A set piece. Just a painted front like something off an old film lot. Behind it: a patchwork of old billboards, rusting nails, and uneven sheets of scrap wood. It was a façade, nothing more.

'Sophie! Come here!'

She appeared around the corner, and her face registered

shock as she took in what I had found. Her eyes flicked from the false wall to me, searching for sense in it.

'This... isn't a real house,' she said, her voice uncertain. I could hear the disappointment beneath the words, echoing my own. All the distance we'd travelled, all the time we'd spent. And for what? A trick.

'Prince!' I shouted as I rounded back to the front.

He was still there, smoking contentedly on the porch, framed perfectly against the illusion. From this angle the façade looked solid—deceptively real.

He looked up at me with the calm detachment of someone who'd seen this moment coming.

'What's the matter?' he asked mildly.

'The house, Prince! It's not real!'

He chuckled, a soft rasp escaping from beneath his pipe.

'Of course it's real, Abe. Just because you think it isn't doesn't make it so. It's right there, isn't it?'

'It's just a set piece! There's nothing behind the door but open desert!'

'Mmm,' he muttered, his voice growing drowsy. 'It's true. You walk around back and you'll see more desert. That's just common sense, Abe. Now why don't you try opening the door... and see what's inside?'

I stepped toward the door, irritation smouldering. This was absurd—he knew as well as I did that the whole thing was an illusion. Sophie came back around to join me, her expression somewhere between amusement and confusion.

'Prince, is this really the Devil's house?' she asked.

Prince grinned, his eyes glinting through the haze of pipe smoke.

'I brought you here, didn't I? That was my job. Now tell your mister to open the door before the sun disappears. Time's short.'

She looked at me.

I stood at the threshold, my hand resting on the silver handle.

'Go on, Abe,' she said softly.

I pushed.

Reality shattered.

Another desert stretched before me—but not the one we knew. It was already night in there. A full moon hung high in a dark violet sky, where the roof of the house should have been. The cracked earth inside was pale and dry, like the bed of a vanished lake, the mud fractured into intricate tessellations that spread endlessly in every direction.

I slammed the door shut, breath short, heart racing.

Behind me, Prince chuckled softly.

Sophie tried to peer past me, but from where she stood she couldn't see through the doorway.

'What is it?' she asked, her face lit with anticipation.

I leaned against the frame, struggling to collect myself.

'It's... somewhere else. Another place entirely. The inside isn't the same as the outside.'

If I'd learnt anything that day, it was that reality had no obligation to behave the way you expected.

I turned to Sophie.

'The sun's getting low,' she said, reading my hesitation.

I didn't want to leave her.

In the golden light she looked radiant—too beautiful, too real. Her eyes, wide and full of emotion, pulled every memory I had of her into a single overwhelming wave of clarity.

I looked at her.

Not as someone in the world...

but as the world itself.

'I'm scared, Sophie!' I cried, the words torn from somewhere deep inside me. 'What if I don't make it back? What if I'm lost to you, swept away in some current of time and space?'

Prince murmured something behind us.

'Time...'

Sophie stepped closer. Her hand found mine. Her cheeks were wet with tears.

‘It won’t happen, Abey. Please... go. Go through the door.’

But I couldn’t ignore the fear. It sat heavy inside my chest.

‘What if it does happen?’ I asked, trembling.

She smiled, though it wavered.

‘Then at least we had today. This incredible day. The best day of my life. I love you, Abe.’

It was the first time she had said it.

And I knew she meant every word.

I choked on my own reply.

‘I love you too. If I don’t make it back... I want you to know... I’ll love you forever.’

Sophie covered her mouth with both hands, her eyes full of everything we had lived... and everything we might lose.

The air thickened with the weight of what was coming.

With one last look into her tear-bright eyes, I turned, pressed down on the silver handle, and stepped through—

just before the sun disappeared beyond the horizon.

It felt like walking through water.

The air was thicker.

Gravity heavier.

Light from our world spilled in behind me.

Then, when I turned—

the doorway was gone.

I stood alone beneath a moon like a silver coin in an ocean of black sky. Its cold light washed over the strange desert, painting the cracked earth in ghostly shades of blue and silver.

The house...

The Devil

Chapter six

O Diabo Invertida

The Devil Reversed

Beyond the doorway, the world was eerily flat—like a tabletop stretching endlessly into the dark. Out on the horizon, vague, jagged shapes hinted at mountains, but they were too distant to offer any real significance. I stepped cautiously away from the house. The ground beneath me crackled, brittle and fragmented, like mud that had once been soaked and then dried too quickly. My footprints pressed into it cleanly, marking a trail away from the doorway and into the unknown.

A few feet ahead, something snaked across the cracked earth.

An electrical cord.

It wound away into the distance.

I squinted, trying to follow its path. Far off, just beyond certainty, a faint glow hovered in the darkness. It might have been a light, but the silver wash of moonlight made it difficult to trust my eyes. Still, curiosity tugged at me. The extension lead disappeared back towards the doorway, plugged neatly into a socket beside it.

Whatever waited at the other end, I knew that was where I needed to go.

So I followed it, tracking its gentle curves across the fractured ground.

The air had been cold inside the house.

Out here it was colder still.

Not windy.

Not biting.

Just... empty.

It felt almost like a vacuum.

I wrapped my arms around myself and kept walking towards the small halo of warm light floating in the darkness.

As I drew closer, I realised it was a tall standing lamp. It stood alone upon the barren earth, its cord coiled at the base like a sleeping serpent. A frosted glass globe cast a warm yellow glow over the little island of light.

Beside it sat a deep red sofa.

And reclining upon it...

was a man.

Fear hit me like a hammer.

A voice—unmistakable, though heard only inside my own mind—rolled across the empty landscape.

Come meet the Devil.

The words tore through me.

Every instinct screamed at me to turn and run.

Instead, I forced myself forward, stepping into the warm pool of lamplight.

I stopped about two metres away.

Outside the lamp's glow there was nothing.

The darkness swallowed everything.

Here, beneath its gentle light, the entire world seemed to revolve around the man before me.

The sofa was exquisite.

Velvet the colour of fresh blood.

Mahogany carved with pastoral scenes.

Its feet ended in tiny human heads, while the arms curled into masks of comedy and tragedy.

He occupied the far end of the two-seater—as though it had been built for whispered conversations rather than comfort.

At first glance he looked almost holy.

A picture-book Jesus.

White robes.

Sandals.

Gentle eyes.

Then the image dissolved.

Before my eyes his appearance shifted effortlessly.

Now he wore a short-sleeved shirt.

Blond hair.

Piercing blue eyes.

A can of beer rested casually in one hand while the other stretched lazily across the back of the couch.

He watched me with unnerving intensity.

Madness danced somewhere behind his smile.

'Hi,' I managed, my voice cracking.

'El Diablo?'

I held out my hand.

He didn't move.

He didn't blink.

Embarrassed, I slowly withdrew it.

He looked perfectly comfortable despite the cold.

Warm.

Confident.

Entirely at ease.

Still he said nothing.

'I... need help,' I continued.

'A representative. Someone to argue my case... and hers.'

The word wife hovered in my mind but refused to come.

Death might dissolve marriage.

It didn't dissolve love.

'There's an organisation. An afterlife committee. They call themselves the Oversight.'

I swallowed.

'Ever heard of them?'

He remained perfectly still.

His silence filled the little circle of light.

'I need someone to renegotiate my agreement with them.'

I shifted awkwardly, trying to stay warm.

When he finally spoke, his voice wasn't what I'd expected.

It wasn't loud.

But it carried enormous weight.

As though the ground itself had decided to speak.

'I've done that sort of thing.'

He patted the empty cushion beside him.

'Come.'

A small smile.

'Tell me your story.'

I hesitated.

Then sat carefully on the edge of the sofa.

'I don't really know where to begin.'

'Start where you feel safest.'

His tone surprised me.

It was kind.

I drew a slow breath.

'About five years ago I started remembering my past life. In those memories I saw Sophie. I'd promised I'd find her again in our next life. So I searched... and today I finally found her.'

He nodded.

Listening.

'But almost immediately a man calling himself the Jackal appeared. He said I'd already fulfilled my agreement. I was allowed one meeting with her. Nothing more.'

I paused.

‘He warned me that my memories would be erased within twenty-four hours. If I tried to see her again… he’d stop me.’

The Devil laughed.

The sound drifted away into the darkness like a stone sinking into deep water.

‘And naturally…’

He smiled.

‘…you ignored him.’

I couldn’t help smiling back.

‘Yes.’

‘You chased after her.’

He counted on his fingers.

‘The Jackal tried to crush you.’

‘You escaped.’

‘You somehow managed to file a formal complaint against the Oversight.’

He laughed again.

‘Not easy, by the way. Those bureaucratic bastards hate paperwork but absolutely adore creating it.’

He leaned back.

‘So now poor Jackal has been benched.’

‘Temporarily.’

'Can you help me?' I asked quietly.

He stretched comfortably.

'It's been a long time since anyone came asking about love.'

He looked almost nostalgic.

'These days it's always money.'

'Power.'

'Youth.'

'Influence.'

'Nobody asks for connection anymore.'

He looked directly at me.

'But you...'

'You want freedom.'

'That's unusual.'

He stood.

With a lazy flick of his fingers, dozens of files shimmered into existence above the cracked earth.

He reached into the impossible stack and pulled free a battered brown folder.

'Let's see what we've got.'

Halfway back to the sofa...

his legs bent the wrong way.

His body shifted without effort.

Dark fur spread across his skin.

His feet became cloven hooves.

Curving horns emerged from his brow.

A mane of coarse black hair ran down his spine.

He settled back onto the sofa.

Entirely naked.

Entirely unconcerned.

His golden eyes had no pupils.

Only age.

If he noticed my discomfort, he gave no sign.

'Let's see...'

He opened the file.

'Childhood sweethearts...'

He nodded thoughtfully.

'Ah.'

His expression darkened.

'Killed during the war.'

He looked up.

'She survived you.'

He held my gaze.

'By sixty years.'

Silence settled between us.

‘Yes,’ I said quietly.

He looked back down.

‘Does she remember?’

‘No.’

‘Does she want to?’

‘I honestly don’t know.’

‘I wanted her to come with me.’

‘I didn’t want to answer for her.’

He closed the folder for a moment.

‘So.’

‘What exactly do you want me to do?’

‘I want a chance.’

‘That’s all.’

‘I want them to leave us alone.’

‘I want us to decide what we are to each other.’

He stroked his chin.

‘She believes you?’

‘About your previous life together?’

‘She does now.’

‘Today changed everything.’

He sighed.

‘Well...’

'I can already tell you what went wrong with your original agreement.'

My stomach tightened.

'What?'

'She survived you.'

Another pause.

'By sixty years.'

'I don't understand.'

'Why does that matter?'

He regarded me patiently.

'Because sixty years is an entire lifetime.'

'You don't know who she became.'

'What she chose.'

'Who she loved.'

'What she regretted.'

'Who she forgave.'

'Those sixty years belong to her.'

I looked away.

'But she doesn't remember.'

He nodded.

'That's the second problem.'

'If she doesn't remember...'

'She can't truly consent.'

'That's what the Oversight exists to protect.'

'The people still asleep.'

I frowned.

'But she asked me to find her.'

'She did.'

'Once.'

He leaned forward.

'But now she's also someone else.'

'Both people exist inside her.'

He let the sentence settle.

'Which one do you want to love?'

My answer came immediately.

'Both.'

A faint smile crossed his face.

'You woke up because you weren't supposed to die.'

He tapped the folder.

'Your death was a fluke.'

He shrugged.

'The system corrected itself.'

'You received one meeting.'

'Balance restored.'

I stared at him.

'You're telling me...'

'They cheated me?'

He smiled sadly.

'Not deliberately.'

'The afterlife isn't neat.'

'It's administration.'

'Endless variables.'

'Mistakes happen.'

'People like me...'

He gestured towards himself.

'...deal in compromise.'

I lowered my head.

Anger slowly dissolved into grief.

'So what now?'

He folded the file closed.

'If you want my help...'

'There's only one honest path.'

He looked directly into my eyes.

'She has to remember.'

'Everything.'

'Not just your life together.'

'The sixty years after you died.'

I stood and began pacing the little island of light.

'But I love her.'

'She loved me.'

'We were meant to be together.'

He watched me quietly.

'You think you were.'

His voice remained gentle.

'But you weren't there.'

'You don't know who she became.'

'Is it fair to ask her to continue a story...'

'...that only one of you remembers?'

I couldn't answer.

'She might not want those memories back.'

He paused.

'And once she remembers...'

'...there's no forgetting them again.'

I turned towards him.

Fear settled inside me.

'Then what choices do I have?'

He looked up.

Ancient.

Calm.

Patient.

'Only two.'

He smiled.

'And only room...'

'...for two different bargains.'

Justice

Chapter seven

Justiça

Justice

This world was heavy—literally. The air pressed against my skin like damp wool. It was silent, stripped of every familiar sound from the life I'd known.

The Satyr lounged on the blood-red sofa, wearing the title of Devil with quiet amusement. His eyes rested on me with patient curiosity, waiting for my next move. His version of reality left me feeling exposed... hollow.

'Okay,' I sighed, lowering myself onto the sofa beside him. 'What are the choices?'

He gave a slow, knowing nod.

'First choice: you walk away now. You've fulfilled your promise to her. You came back. You recovered a piece of what was lost. Now you spend your final hours with Sophie, and that's it. No more. She forgets everything. You'll remember, but she won't. They call it even. The Jackal is taken off your back. No further consequences.'

'We forget we ever met?' I asked, my voice dry.

'No,' he said gently. 'You'll remember. She won't. You'll carry the weight. You'll have to stay away from her for the rest of your life.'

He paused.

'Think of it as the stitch over the wound you tore open when you tried to wake her.'

The idea of losing her again—of seeing her, holding her, only to disappear from her world forever—made my chest tighten.

'At least,' he continued, 'you get to have it all again, Abe. Even if it's only for a few hours.'

A faint smile.

'A guarantee.'

'No risk.'

I felt cold.

Brittle.

'And the second choice?'

'She remembers everything. All of it. After that, she chooses her own path. Whatever she wants. You're given a reprieve—provided you follow the new rules. You don't wake anyone else, for example.'

'And there's a chance...'

I hesitated.

'There's a chance she won't choose me?'

'Of course.'

He shrugged lightly.

'You had choices when you woke. You chose your path.'

'So will she.'

I nodded, though the truth stung. It had never felt like I'd been choosing.

'So, Abe...'

His voice softened.

'Do you think she loved you enough?'

A pause.

'Do you think she still does?'

The question lodged deep inside my chest.

I'd never doubted before.

I'd always believed she'd love me again, just as she once had.

But the Satyr...

this ancient creature everyone insisted on calling the Devil...

had planted something poisonous inside me.

Doubt.

What had sixty years without me done to her?

Had she carried our promise through time?

Held onto it like a lifeline?

Or had she done what anyone would have done?

Built another life.

Loved someone else.

Raised children.

Forgotten the frightened young man who'd promised to find her again.

Could I blame her if she had?

My heart buckled beneath questions I couldn't answer.

And what about this life?

Today all she knew was that I'd found her.

That I loved her.

That I'd crossed impossible worlds just to keep a promise.

But what if remembering meant discovering another love entirely?

A husband.

A family.

A lifetime built after I was gone.

If you spend most of your life with someone...

doesn't that matter more?

I had to choose.

A few perfect hours with her.

Or a lifetime that might not include me.

How deep did my love really run?

Was it only love if she chose me back?

The Satyr simply watched.

He'd seen this decision made countless times before.

'If you choose the first option,' he said quietly, 'simply walk back through the doorway. She'll be waiting at the house. I'll handle the paperwork.'

A tiny smile.

'You'll spend your final hours together beneath the desert sky.'

'Tomorrow morning they'll take her.'

'She won't remember.'

'She'll be safe.'

'And if I choose the second?'

'Then I go to her.'

'I wake her.'

'I explain everything.'

'Then she decides.'

He looked directly at me.

'And whatever she chooses...'

'...you must accept it.'

'If she wishes to forget again...'

'...you let her go.'

'No searching.'

'No interference.'

'But if she chooses you...'

He smiled.

'I'll take her somewhere safe to wait for you.'

'The Oversight will withdraw.'

'The Jackal disappears.'

'You'll both be free.'

He reached into the empty air beside him.

A thick leather-bound book appeared in his hands.

He rested it gently across his knees.

'Everything's in here.'

He patted the cover.

'Contracts.'

'Once you've decided...'

'...we'll sign on the dotted line.'

My throat tightened.

There was no safety net.

The first choice guaranteed I'd see Sophie again.

She'd remain untouched.

Safe.

The second...

The second meant truth.

Risk.

The possibility she'd remember everything...

and still walk away.

Without giving me the chance to say goodbye.

Unless...

Unless she still loved me.

Then perhaps we'd earned another chance.

Another lifetime.

I closed my eyes.

Then opened them again.

'I want her to choose.'

The Satyr nodded slowly.

'I didn't think you'd take the first offer.'

He closed the book.

'But there is one more matter.'

A smile slowly spread across his face.

'Payment.'

My mouth went dry.

‘For my services.’

‘What’s the price?’ I asked quietly.

He steepled his fingers.

Thoughtful.

Patient.

Calculating.

Finally, he looked at me with calm certainty.

‘Three pounds of flesh.’

A beat.

‘And I’ll have to carve it myself.’

Another beat.

‘Otherwise the transaction doesn’t count.’

The Fool

Chapter eight

O tolo

The Fool

'What?' I stammered. 'You're joking.'

'I'm afraid not.' The Satyr smiled cheerfully, as though he were discussing dinner plans. 'I used to deal in blood, but these days... only flesh will do.'

There was nowhere else to go.

I needed him.

Without his help, there would be no renegotiation. No reprieve. Even if I tried to escape, the Oversight—and the Jackal—would eventually catch up with me.

Our deadline was closing in.

What would Sophie and I do if the Jackal were let loose again? I didn't know how long I had spent in this strange, heavy layer of reality with El Diablo, but I knew one thing.

I had no choice.

'Look,' he added, his tone almost apologetic, 'if you don't agree to the payment, I can't help you.'

I must have looked pale. He clapped me on the back in a poor attempt at reassurance.

'Don't worry. You won't die. You can't die here. Not in this dimension. And the flesh I take grows back.'

He paused.

'Eventually.'

He moved his fingers through the air, miming regeneration.

'Your body feels physical, I know. But out here? You're more energy than matter. Like smoke pretending to be stone.'

His grin stretched wider.

I no longer believed he was anything close to benevolent.

'I need the energy to perform what's required. Part of it is for the contract. Part of it is... personal. Three pounds should do. One for you, one for Sophie, and one for me.'

He shrugged.

'Equal exchange.'

Another smile.

'It will hurt, though. Just as it would on a denser plane. Sorry.'

The blood drained from my face.

I thought of Sophie.

Of the promise I had made.

'Okay,' I said quietly, surrendering to the inevitable.

'Splendid!'

He sprang to his feet, seized my hand and led me away from the warm glow of the lamp and the illusion of safety it offered.

We walked in silence for what felt like hours. The warm circle of lamplight behind us grew smaller with every step until it became another fallen star resting on the desert floor. The ground rose gently beneath our feet, and when we reached the crest of a low hill, something waited there.

A rough stone table.

Worn.

Stained.

Ancient.

Only as I drew closer did I realise what it really was.

An altar.

The Satyr reached beneath it and pulled out a long, coarse rope.

‘Hold out your hands.’

I obeyed.

He bound them tightly, then wound the rope around my torso and legs until I was completely immobilised.

‘Apologies for the restraints,’ he said. ‘People tend to thrash while I’m collecting payment.’

He tightened one final knot.

‘Makes things... messy.’

Then the reality of what was about to happen struck like a blade.

‘Shit. Isn’t there another way?’ I gasped. ‘Please... don’t do this.’

My voice trembled.

My entire body did.

The Satyr lifted me effortlessly and placed me upon the altar’s cold stone surface.

At the head of the table stood a pair of golden scales.

One side had already been stacked with weights.

‘Most people panic around now,’ he muttered.

He began loading more onto the tray.

‘But this part?’

Another weight fell with a deafening clang.

‘Just a technicality.’

The tray slammed down.

Three pounds had never looked so heavy.

'Would you like to bite on this?'

He held up a worn leather strap, almost chewed through at the centre.

My stomach lurched.

I retched dryly before I could answer.

'Okay...'

I struggled for breath.

'I can't do this.'

He said nothing.

We were no longer alone.

Beings of light began appearing around the hill.

They did not arrive.

They unfolded from the air itself, as though the atmosphere could no longer contain them.

Their forms pulsed and shimmered, each blazing with a brilliance that bordered on unbearable. They hovered just above the earth, their bodies in constant motion—a shifting geometry of limbs and wings that multiplied and dissolved within the same instant. Their skin, if it could be called that, was translucent, alive with currents of gold and white fire.

Their bodies were covered in countless eyes—some vast

and unblinking, others no larger than grains of sand.

All watching.

All aware.

Wherever their gaze fell, the air bent and hummed, vibrating with an otherworldly frequency that raised the hairs along my arms. They moved with perfect stillness, suspended in the thin, luminous space between breath and silence.

Then, in unison, they turned towards the Satyr.

Their voices were not spoken.

They were felt.

A chorus reverberated through the ground and into my bones. They called the Satyr by names I could not understand, syllables that shimmered and fractured the air itself. Names I instinctively knew I was forbidden to repeat.

He drew a long, ornate dagger.

The blade gleamed hungrily beneath the moon, humming with an energy I could feel in my teeth.

Silence fell.

I bit down on the strap and braced myself.

The Satyr turned me onto my side, pulled down my trousers and lifted my shirt and jacket. Cold air kissed the exposed stretch of skin from my ribcage to my knee.

The scales above me vibrated softly.

Hungry for balance.

His hands were rough and clinical as they pressed along my torso, searching for a suitable cut.

When the blade touched my flesh, panic tore through me.

Even bound, I twisted instinctively.

'Now, now,' he murmured. 'Almost done.'

Then he plunged the blade into my thigh.

The pain hit like lightning—white-hot and endless.

I screamed into the strap, tears flooding my eyes.

The blade carved downwards.

Metal shrieked against bone.

The pain did not stop.

He sliced slowly along my femur until he reached my knee. Then, with one violent jerk, he tore the blade free.

Blood sprayed across the stone like red ink from a shattered pen.

The agony kept going.

He lifted the severed piece of flesh.

Quivering.

Dripping.

He placed it reverently upon the scale.

The weighted side jerked upwards.

But the scales did not balance.

'Hmm.'

His eyes gleamed with unnatural light.

'Still short.'

Only then did I realise he had changed.

He towered above me now.

Three times the size he had been before.

A mountain of horn, muscle and shadow.

With one enormous hand, he held me against the altar.

The other brought the blade down again.

This time into my back.

He cut with the practised ease of a butcher.

I felt flesh separate from bone as he carved another thick wedge from my body.

My vision blurred.

I felt hollow.

My blood rushed out too quickly.

For one strange moment, I thought I was floating.

Leaving the altar.

Leaving the world.

Through the haze, I saw a familiar face.

The angry little man from outside the RAD stood at the edge of the hill, watching with an unreadable expression.

The Satyr slapped the second piece of flesh onto the scale.

The trays shifted.

Balanced.

'Aha!' he declared. 'Perfect.'

Blood dripped steadily from the loaded plate.

He took a plain bowl and gathered some of it, then dipped a wide brush into the dark red liquid.

With swift, deliberate strokes, he painted symbols and words into the contract book he had shown me earlier.

The terms of our new agreement.

At the edge of my vision, a small dark shape appeared.

Edward.

Madame Bea's cat-shaped familiar.

He padded towards us, sneering as though my suffering had been a personal inconvenience. With casual disdain, he took the contract book from the Satyr's hands.

Then he leapt into the air and—

pop—

vanished into the ether like a warping frog.

The Satyr looked down at me, thoroughly satisfied.

'There you go,' he said brightly. 'All done.'

He clapped his hands together.

'You can get up now.'

Still in shock, I lifted my hands.

The ropes were gone.

I ran trembling fingers along my thigh.

My back.

No wounds.

No blood.

But the pain remained.

The memory of it lived inside me.

The hill had vanished.

The altar was gone.

The beings of light had disappeared.

I was lying on the red sofa again beneath the familiar black lamp.

I gasped, shaking uncontrollably.

'Fuck!' I shouted. 'I'm okay. I'm okay...'

The Satyr beamed down at me, cheerful as ever.

'Payment received,' he said, like a man ticking a box on a form.

36

111

6	32	3	34	35	1
31	7	9	2	4	36
30	8	28	27	11	5
13	29	24	10	12	26
19	14	16	23	22	15
20	21	17	18	25	6

Part Four

THE SILENT DANCE OF STARS

The awakening beyond memory — where silence remembers its own name.

The hum builds to a shriek...

then silence.

She glows—

faintly...

feverishly...

the seed of creation sealed inside her.

He stumbles back,

blackened

and perfect.

Beneath them,

the soil stirs...

ready to receive them once more.

The Sun

Chapter one

O Sol Invertida

The Sun Reversed

The Satyr—so often mistaken for the Devil—was practically radiant with delight. He licked his hand and slicked down his wild mane, trying to tame it into something resembling order. Watching him preen like a vain teenager was almost surreal.

I leaned back into the sofa, running my fingers over the places where my wounds should have been. They still throbbed with phantom pain—scars and welts raised like ridges across my skin, raw and tingling, though no open cuts remained. The memory of the blade cutting into me was seared into my nerves. I would never forget it.

At last, the Satyr turned to me, ready.

'So,' he said, that devilish grin spreading across his face, 'I'll leave you here. When everything's in place, I'll contact you. Got it?'

I simply stared back at him, too drained to answer with anything but silence. We were in different dimensions—how the hell was he planning to reach me? I decided that was his problem to solve.

'Yes,' I finally said, though my voice trembled. I was terrified. I had handed my heart—and our fate—over to Sophie. Would she choose me? My mind reeled.

'Will you tell me what she decides?'

'No.' He watched me from the edge of the lamp's halo. 'I'll only call when the deal is sealed. You'll go to a place you've chosen. If she shows up, she chose you. If not... you'll have your answer.'

My stomach sank. Blood drained from my face.

'Okay,' I whispered. 'So I won't know until I go there?'

He nodded solemnly.

'That's how it has to be. Will you be okay?'

I nodded again, barely.

'So... where should the meeting place be, Abe? You choose.'

My head throbbed. I thought back over the day's long journey with her.

'The Pimple,' I said.

'The what?'

'A butte. We climbed it earlier. It's close to the black house. It meant something.'

He gave a short nod.

'Very well.'

He stepped backwards and bowed slightly.

'I go to serve your will.'

As he disappeared into the darkness, a strange vulnerability overtook me. I squinted into the void, but the lamplight made it difficult to see, so I reached over and switched it off.

Moonlight flooded the desert.

In its pale silver glow, I watched him making his way towards the ruined house. A brief flash of light burst from the doorway as he opened it to the natural world.

My heart ached.

Somewhere beyond that door, Sophie was waiting.

Or she wasn't.

I slumped back onto the sofa.

There was no other choice I could have made.

I wouldn't blame her if she'd moved on—fallen in love again, married, perhaps even had children.

After all...

I had died.

But this hadn't been a test.

I wasn't trying to prove her love.

I wasn't trying to prove mine.

Love had finally demanded something of me.

It had asked me to let go.

Something inside me had changed.

Surrender had never been part of my nature.

Yet even if she didn't choose me...

I would still love her.

Forever.

For infinity.

The truth struck me with startling clarity.

That afternoon in the park, all those years ago, when I promised I would love her always...

I hadn't understood what those words truly meant.

I'd been young.

Idealistic.

But even then...

I'd spoken the truth.

I loved her across lifetimes.

Not because she loved me.

But simply because she existed.

And now I wanted her love freely given.

No coercion.

No magic.

No bargains.

The epiphany hit me like a blow.

I had loved selfishly once—with expectations, with conditions. Somewhere along the way, they had fallen away. Stripped from me in a single act of surrender.

I lay broken upon the blood-red sofa, bleeding invisibly into the silence surrounding me.

I don't know how long I stayed there.

It felt like eternity.

In reality, it was probably twenty minutes.

Then came the ringing.

Shrill.

Insistent.

I fumbled until I found the source—an old-fashioned telephone perched on a side table. It vibrated as it rang. I snatched up the receiver, almost dropping it in my haste.

'Hello?' I gasped.

The Satyr's voice crackled through the static, metallic and final.

'Abe Mendes. It's done. Good luck. Godspeed.'

A loud click.

Nothing more.

He was gone.

The handset slipped from my fingers and slammed against the table, emitting a harsh, disconnected tone.

My thoughts spiralled.

Had I just been given a second chance...

...or a second death?

I left the receiver where it hung and stumbled towards the dark silhouette of the house.

Towards the door.

Towards whatever waited beyond it.

I hoped Sophie would be there.

Waiting for me on the summit of the Pimple.

But somewhere deep inside, I suspected she wouldn't.

Still...

I had to try.

Every step felt heavier than the last, as though I were pushing through invisible water. My scars burned as though freshly opened. The memory of the knife still lived inside my body.

I reached the door.

Pulled it open.

And there it was.

The real world.

The desert air rushed over me all at once—cold, clean, alive with scents and sounds that simply hadn't existed in the world beyond the door.

I stepped forward.

Reborn.

My legs buckled beneath me.

Sweat poured from every pore.

I caught myself on the veranda's railing before I fell.

Prince sat nearby, rocking gently in his chair, his pipe glowing softly in the darkness. The sweet scent of cherry tobacco drifted lazily across the cool night air.

The sun had long since disappeared.

Night belonged to the desert now.

Prince looked younger somehow.

'What time is it?' I asked.

'Eleven o'clock,' he replied between slow puffs. 'The master came out. Took your girl. Spoke with her about you.'

I lowered myself onto the porch beside him, resting my back against the wall.

'Have you ever loved someone, Prince?'

He set his pipe down carefully.

A single wrinkle deepened across his brow.

'I have,' he said softly. 'I've loved many women.'

A gentle smile crossed his face.

'Not all of them loved me back.'

Neither of us spoke for a while.

'There was one,' he continued. 'When I was young.'

His eyes drifted towards the desert.

'We had everything we needed for a good life. Real love.'

He smiled to himself.

'I asked her to come away with me. Offered her everything.'

A pause.

'She said no.'

'No explanation?'

Prince slowly shook his head.

'Just... no.'

Silence settled between us again.

'I went home,' he said eventually. 'Restless. Haunted by her memory.'

He looked down at his hands.

'One day I met the Devil at a crossroads. Long before he had this place. Back then he travelled the roads selling tonics, snake oil... whatever kept food on the table.'

A sad smile.

'I begged him to change her heart.'

'And?'

'He refused.'

Prince looked at me then.

Really looked.

'I think he knew what would happen.'

Our eyes met.

In that moment we understood each other completely.

'We were the same,' I whispered.

He nodded.

'The master asked me to tell you something.'

I waited.

'Everything is as you both agreed.'

He gestured towards my Mini.

'I filled your tank. More than enough to reach the mountain.'

I climbed slowly to my feet.

We shook hands.

He gripped mine tightly.

'Good luck, Abe.'

I started towards the car.

Then stopped.

There was one question I still needed answered.

I turned back.

'He warned you that you'd regret it.'

Prince nodded.

'Do you?'

He looked at the desert for a very long time.

'Not a single day passes without wishing I'd left her alone.'

His voice barely carried above the breeze.

'I begged him every day until he finally gave in.'

His shoulders sagged.

'He used his magic.'

A long silence.

'She came.'

A smile flickered across his face.

'For a little while... she smiled.'

The smile disappeared.

'Then the sadness arrived.'

His voice cracked.

'Slowly.'

'Like a sickness of the soul.'

I stood perfectly still.

'I tried everything. I sang to her. Held her. Promised her the world.'

His eyes closed.

'But I'd taken the one thing she truly wanted.'

'I know,' I said quietly.

He looked at me.

'Do you?'

I nodded.

'Freedom.'

Prince smiled the saddest smile I had ever seen.

'Freedom.'

He swallowed hard.

'One day I left to find him again. I wanted to undo what I'd done.'

His voice broke.

'When we came back... it was too late.'

He stared into the darkness.

'She'd hanged herself above our camp.'

He began to cry.

Not loudly.

Not dramatically.

Just quietly.

Like a man who had run out of tears decades ago.

'I lost her either way, Abe.'

His voice sounded like gravel dragged across stone.

'Either way... she left me.'

He slumped back into the rocking chair.

Older again.

Smaller somehow.

The night slowly gathered around him.

I apologised into the silence between us.

Thanked him one final time.

I stood there a moment longer.

Then I turned and walked towards the Mini.

In the rear-view mirror, I watched Prince...

...and the black house...

...disappear into the endless darkness of the desert.

The HangingMan

Chapter two

O Homem Enforcado

The Hanging Man

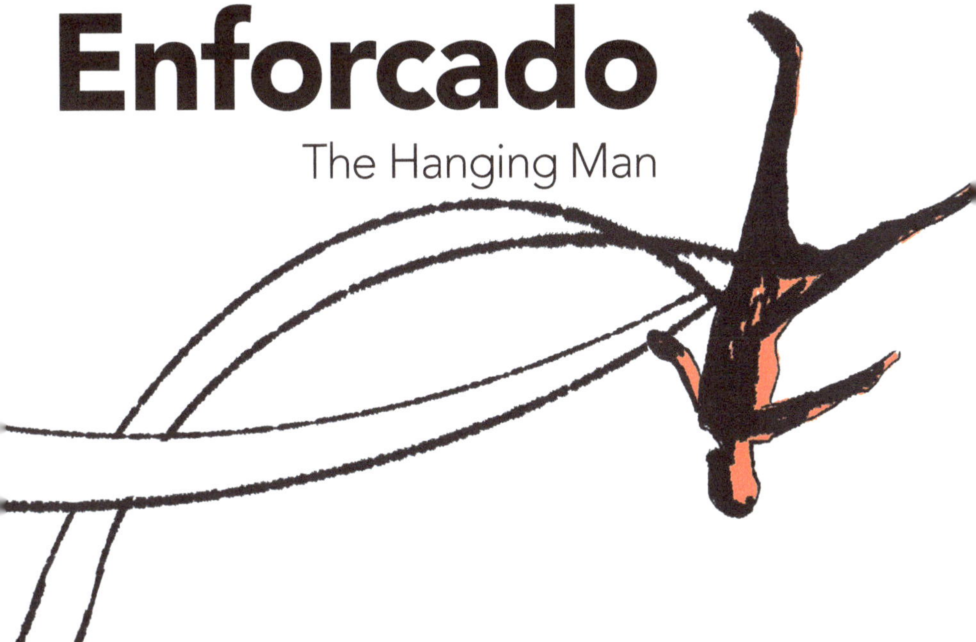

The drive back along the dirt road was a lonely one. The only light came from my car's headlamps, twin beams carving into the unknown, revealing just enough of the winding track ahead to keep moving forward. I leaned into the wheel, eyes fixed on the cones of illumination as they carved through the dusty wilderness. Beyond them, the night pressed in—dense and impenetrable, like black molasses filling every space the car left behind.

When I glanced through the side windows, all I could make out was the faint ridge of sand lining the road, rising into banks that hemmed me in. The comforting vastness of the desert had vanished, swallowed by darkness. The track twisted and curled with a mind of its own, like a living thing, challenging me at every bend. Frustrated and exhausted, I took the corners too fast, skidding dangerously across the loose gravel.

More than an hour passed like that—hunched over the wheel, my neck stiff, my eyes aching. Finally, I slammed on the brakes. The tyres shrieked as the Mini slid sideways before coming to rest in a plume of dust. I killed the engine.

Killed the lights.

Silence.

Stepping out into the predawn cold, I breathed in the stillness. It had to be past one in the morning—technically a new day—but the darkness felt eternal. As my eyes adjusted, the desert slowly emerged from the void. I climbed onto the bonnet of the Mini and lay back against the windscreen, letting the quiet settle inside me.

Even here, in the heart of the desert, the difference between the Satyr's dimension inside the Black House and my own world was unmistakable. That place had been empty, suffocating, unreal. Here, there was texture, life, scent—the thick aroma of dust mingling with the sharp bite of early dew. The earth had begun to cool, and moisture clung to the sand, lifting some of the dryness from the air.

Crickets sang in chaotic rhythm. Somewhere in the distance, a coyote howled—a solitary voice in the silence. It reminded me how flat and lifeless that other world had been.

But most breathtaking of all was the night sky above me.

The stars unveiled themselves slowly. First a handful.

Then hundreds.

Then thousands.

Until the heavens blazed with ancient light.

They didn't twinkle.

They burned.

The Milky Way stretched across the sky like a luminous road, pointing through the desert towards the looming silhouette of the Pimple.

My destination.

My reckoning.

I lay there longer than I should have, thinking about what waited ahead. I'd made my choice—one I could live with. I felt as though I'd died again, suspended between two worlds. Like the day I'd floated above the battlefield, weightless and untethered, drawn towards a stairway leading somewhere beyond.

But this time...

I might not be alone at the end.

She might be there.

Sophie.

Waiting.

Perhaps we could still walk away from all this together.

Back inside the car, I didn't switch the lights on. I didn't need them. The road was there, and I followed it through the darkness until I reached the highway. Only then did I flick the headlamps back to life.

This was the final leg of a journey that had begun five years earlier.

I shivered.

It didn't seem possible that the search could finally be ending.

One way or another.

The highway lay empty ahead of me. No barriers. No bends. Nothing to slow me down. I buried my foot on the accelerator, chasing the stars as they dipped towards the horizon, guiding me to the dark shape of the butte waiting in the distance.

For a while, I wasn't Abe Mendes anymore.

I was something older.

An ancient mariner steering by the constellations, trusting only the truth of the stars.

After another hour racing through the darkness, the shape of the Pimple swallowed the sky, blotting out the frozen fire beyond it. I reached the same place where Sophie and I had stood barely fifteen hours earlier, veering off the road and skidding into the sandy shoulder beside the highway.

Before the engine had even finished ticking itself cool, I was already out of the car, striding towards the mountain without looking back.

I tilted my head towards the summit.

It loomed above me.

Massive.

Flat-topped.

Waiting.

My final climb.

Then I was climbing.

The slope was treacherous, the loose earth collapsing beneath my boots. I scrambled, slipped and clawed my way upwards through the darkness. It wasn't like before.

It was harder.

Every step burned.

But one thought kept pulling me upwards.

Maybe she'd be there.

Sophie.

As she had been in another life.

Yet doubt gnawed constantly at the edges of hope.

I stopped often, bent double, lungs burning in the freezing air. When I'd begun climbing, the dashboard clock had read 3:45 a.m. I had no idea whether I'd reach the summit before dawn spilled across the desert.

Still I climbed.

Hands digging into the earth.

Feet searching desperately for purchase.

Then—

my fingers struck stone.

The cold, sharp face of the butte.

Relief surged through me.

Closely followed by dread.

I'd aimed blindly for the narrow chute Sophie and I had climbed before—the only route I knew.

Somehow...

impossibly...

I'd found it again.

I laughed.

Half disbelief.

Half triumph.

Then collapsed at the foot of the cliff.

Above me rose more than two hundred metres of near-vertical rock.

The final ascent.

The last truth.

I leaned back against the cold stone, trembling with exhaustion and anticipation.

Then, without warning, nausea seized me.

I doubled over and vomited into the dirt.

When I straightened again, every hair on the back of my neck stood upright.

I knew that feeling.

Someone else was here.

Justice

Chapter three

Justiça Invertida

Justice Reversed

'What's the matter, son?'

The Jackal crouched just a few metres above me, perched in the gully like a predator sizing up a wounded animal. His pale skin shimmered faintly in the growing half-light. The horizon blushed with the first hint of dawn, but it was still too dark to see him clearly.

Except for those eyes.

Burning red.

Slicing through me.

I swallowed, my throat too dry to answer.

'What's that? You choking on your tongue, bruv?' He let out a rasping wheeze of a laugh, a sound twisted and hollow, like death mocking hope.

'What are you doing here?' I croaked at last.

'Made a deal, didn't you?' he said, cutting me off. 'Yeah, yeah. With Pan. I know. Word got around. You're outta my hands now. Made me all misty, bruv—couldn't even say goodbye. So I figured I'd drop in, offer my congrats. You slipped the leash. Doesn't happen often. Bravo.'

He spread his arms towards the waking sky with theatrical delight.

'But... will you get the girl?'

His smile widened.

'You think the sky is still, Abe. That those bright fires above us are fixed in their places, keeping faithful watch. But listen more closely—listen with the marrow, not the ear—and you'll hear it. A shiver. A sway. A dance too vast for human eyes to grasp. That is where we walk now, you and I: in the space between steps, in the hush between heartbeats, where silence is louder than the thrum of war drums.'

He burst into laughter again, high and deranged. It rattled down the slope like broken glass.

'If I'm not yours anymore, then why the fuck are you

here?' I snapped. My patience with him had long since burned away.

The laughter stopped.

His eyes flared again, like fresh coals catching fire.

'I don't like your tone, Abe.'

He hissed my name like a curse.

'Sure, I got no orders now. No leash on you. But that don't mean I ain't still me. I still hate your guts. And now?'

He smiled.

'No rules.'

Another step.

'No protocol.'

One more.

'Just you and me.'

He dropped lightly onto the slope beside me.

'One-on-one.'

Before I could react, his hand clamped around my throat. He lifted me effortlessly and slammed me against the cold cliff face. My spine jarred violently against the rock. Saliva dripped from between the jagged rows of his teeth.

'First, I break you,' he growled into my ear.

His grin became monstrous.

'Then I'll drag your girl up that cliff... and I'll make sure you hear every scream.'

His breath smelt of rot.

My stomach lurched.

Blind with fury, I drove my knee upwards with everything I had.

It smashed into his chest.

The Jackal staggered backwards.

I crashed to the ground but forced myself upright, lungs burning, and threw myself straight at him.

'You only ever had power because you couldn't be killed, you coward!'

My boot connected with his face.

His head snapped backwards.

He snarled.

His claws ripped across my shoulder and arm.

White-hot pain exploded through me.

Blood sprayed across the rocks.

I staggered...

...but I didn't fall.

'No powers this time,' he sneered. 'Just flesh and blood.'

He licked his lips.

'But you, Abey...'

Another step.

'You ain't got it in you to finish me.'

His grin widened.

'Me?'

He laughed.

'I love killing.'

He came at me.

Fast.

I barely had time to brace.

My boots slammed into his chest as he collided with me.

I shoved with everything I had.

He flew backwards down the slope.

I threw myself after him without thinking.

We tumbled through dust and stone, limbs tangled together.

My hand clawed blindly through the dirt.

Searching.

Until it found it.

A rock.

Heavy.

Solid.

I dragged it with me.

We smashed into a boulder.

The impact stunned us both.

As we struggled onto our knees, he sank his teeth into my arm and drove a fist into my ribs.

My vision blurred.

I screamed.

Grabbed a fistful of his hair.

Raised the rock.

Brought it down across his face.

Blood burst into the dawn.

He reeled.

I hit him again.

Again.

Again.

He slid backwards down the slope.

Dazed.

Bleeding.

I didn't stop.

I launched myself onto his chest, riding him down the hillside, hammering the rock into his skull over and over.

'DIE, YOU PSYCHOTIC FUCK!'

Blood soaked my hands.

His body slackened beneath me.

His limbs twitched once.

Like a crushed insect.

Then...

Nothing.

Panting, shaking, I stumbled away from him.

The rock slipped from my fingers.

I paced in a crooked circle, trying to catch my breath.

Then I looked back.

He wasn't fading.

He wasn't disappearing.

He was dead.

A dark stain spread slowly beneath his shattered head.

I had killed him.

Again.

But this time...

It was final.

There was no triumph.

No relief.

Only the cold ache of survival.

I wiped the blood from my face and examined the deep gouges across my shoulder and arm. Every movement burned.

Above me, the narrow cleft in the cliff waited.

I didn't look back.

I climbed.

Below me, the world lay wrapped in the quiet hush before dawn.

Above...

My fate was waiting.

The World

Chapter four

O Mundo

The World

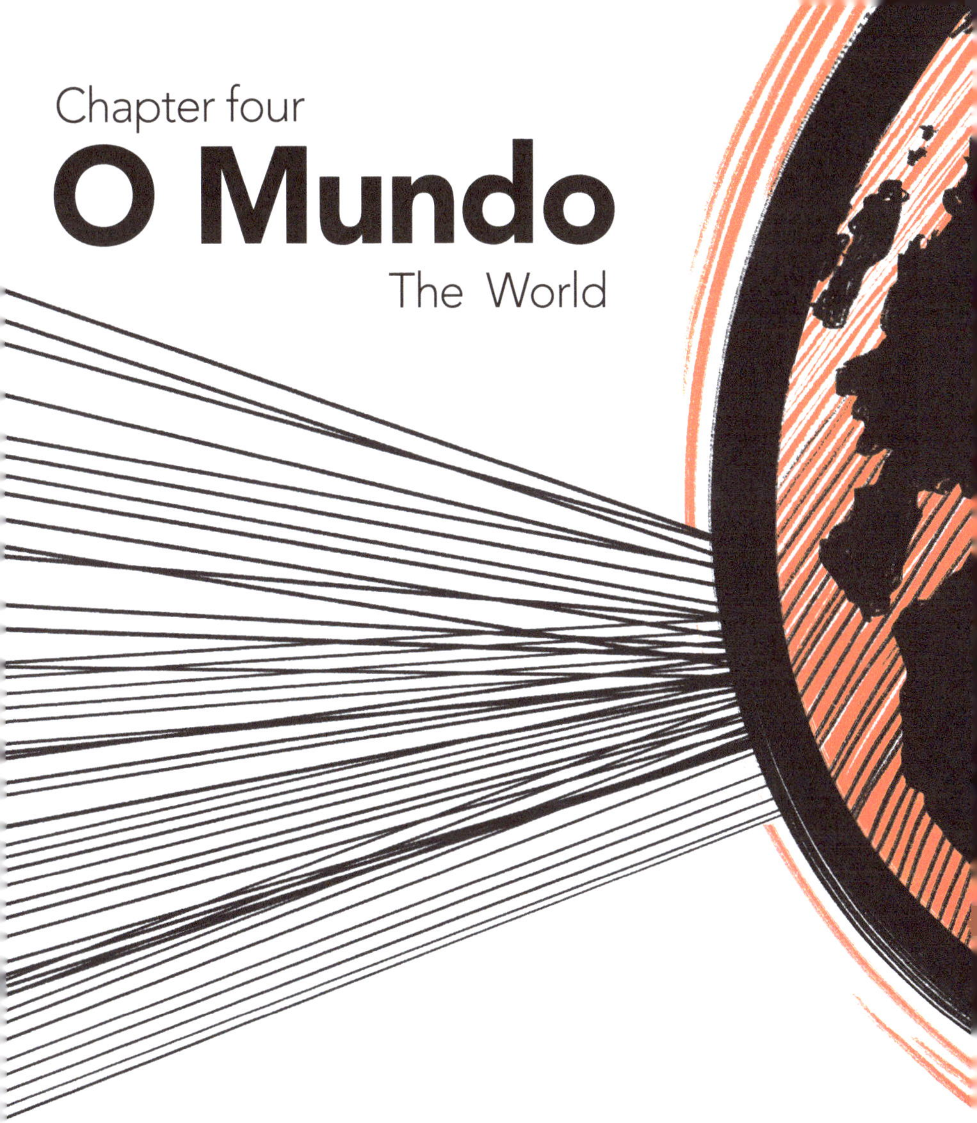

I had reached the top of the butte.

Every ounce of strength had drained from me, but I pulled myself over the final ledge and collapsed onto the flat summit. Above, the stars still burned across the heavens.

Ancient.

Unreachable.

For a fleeting moment, their beauty lifted my heart, but dawn was coming quickly. The sun, already edging over the horizon, would soon erase all but the brightest.

The memories loosened their grip, fading like lantern light swallowed by dawn.

Below me lay the memory of killing the Jackal, right there on the slope where I had ended him. It lingered like a shadow at the edge of my vision, but even that was beginning to fade. The other memories I had so carefully pieced together were gone too, scattered into the silence.

Here, at the summit of the butte, the desert came back into focus: the same vast quilt of ochres and reds breathing beneath me, the same low hum of drums drifting from the camp below.

The festival still stirred. Figures moved faintly in the half-light, their laughter carrying on the cooling air. A few lanterns continued to climb skywards, red sparks rising into the slowly brightening blue.

But something had shifted.

The desert, the sky, the flicker of firelight—it was all as before, yet not. Every grain of sand seemed charged with what had passed through me, with what could never again be unseen. The silence between sounds pressed closer, vast and knowing. Time, once fractured, folded in upon itself.

I was back.

Breathing the same air.

Standing where I had ended up.

I rose, panting, and searched the summit for her.

Nothing.

I staggered towards the place where Sophie and I had sat, our legs swinging over the edge. The eastern sky had begun to glow. The first sliver of sun blazed like a blade, cutting through the darkness and casting its golden fire across the land.

The starlight faded.

I sank onto the cold stone and looked upwards, trying to catch one final glimpse of infinity before daylight erased it.

She wasn't there.

And I would never know why.

All I had left was myself.

All I had begun with was myself.

I let my thoughts drift as the sky changed around me, blooming with violets and soft yellow-gold. The sun possessed its own kind of majesty.

Love, I realised, is not something you possess.

Not even an emotion.

It is an exchange.

An encounter between souls.

An ever-shifting force reaching into every part of existence, from the physical to the divine.

Some people burn together longer than others. Some never fade. Their love remains clear and whole, like a constant signal running through the noise of existence.

Others flicker.

Flare.

Then disappear.

But some loves are older than flesh.

Some flames survive death itself.

Like the stars above, still burning long after they have disappeared from sight.

I still loved her.

Sophie.

Even in her absence, I loved her completely.

For reasons I might never understand, she had chosen not to meet me. Instead, she had let me go, allowing me to drift from her orbit.

Yet the truth I had started with remained unchanged.

I loved.

That had never been the problem.

With a sigh, I rose, bruised, battered and bleeding, and turned towards the furrow in the rock. I took one last look at the awakening sky and the vast desert stretching beneath it.

Then I began the descent.

The pain in my chest eclipsed the wounds across my body.

But there was peace too.

A strange, quiet peace.

No regret.

I had loved her as well as I could.

Without conditions.

With everything I possessed.

And I had kept my promise.

As I moved down the steep, sandy slope, I thought of her not with bitterness, but with hope. I wished for her happiness. And if, through some miracle of time or fate, our paths crossed again in a distant life, I hoped I could show her the full depth of what I still carried for her.

This is the brutal truth of life:

We are born to die.

We are not the flowers, brief and beautiful.

We are the tree.

The whole tree.

Roots, trunk, bud and bloom.

With every season, we emerge, flower, fade and fall. But something within us continues.

Something eternal.

We are waves crashing upon a beach for one brief moment before returning to the ocean from which we came.

We are travellers.

We are star-walkers.

Sometimes, we find each other along the journey. And when we do, if we are fortunate, we walk side by side.

For a while.

Eventually, we are drawn back into whatever lies beyond.

I reached the Mini, having slid most of the way down the slope. Covered in dust and blood, I opened the door and turned back.

The butte loomed behind me, quiet and strange in the morning light.

I had died upon that hill.

And resurrected myself.

I had learnt to let go.

Because, in the end, nothing holds forever. Not pain.

Not joy. Not even love as we understand it.

What matters—what remains—is how we choose to carry those we have loved.

What we choose to become after everything else has fallen away.

At some point, we all face the impossible.

But within that fire, we can find compassion.

Compassion for one another, because we all bleed.

We all break.

We all lose.

I was ready.

Ready to live again.

Epilogue

About ten miles down the road towards Memphis, I spotted the dark silhouette of something familiar on the verge.

No bloody way…

It couldn't be…

Was that…?

I slowed to a stop and peered at the inky figure sitting on the sandy embankment a few feet from the roadside. The soil glowed a reddish hue in the early morning sunshine, and the black cat regarded me with its usual look of sarcastic superiority.

I stepped out of the car and walked a few paces closer, studying its sleek ebony coat.

'Edward? Is that you?'

The cat didn't answer. It stretched languidly, yawned widely, and sauntered past me towards the open passenger window. With effortless grace, it leapt into the seat. By the time I reached the car, it was seated comfortably, licking its front paw as though nothing unusual had occurred.

I could hardly believe what I was seeing.

What did Edward want?

And where was Madame Bea?

I stood there for a moment, rubbing my chin, then shrugged and slid into the driver's seat beside the silent cat.

'Let me guess,' I said. 'Your magical transport potion's run out, and you need a lift back to Memphis?'

Edward gave me a sidelong, sardonic sneer that made it abundantly clear I had guessed wrong.

I let my forehead fall onto the steering wheel.

'Look!' I snapped. 'I've had enough of you strange fairy creatures barging into my life. Either you tell me what the hell is going on, or you get out.'

I gestured towards the embankment with my left hand.

My determination seemed to work.

Edward began to morph, his form growing and shifting into something more familiar—a squat, furry figure, part-cat, part-human, with tiny hands and upright legs.

Then came his voice.

'All right, all right, don't get your knickers in a twist!' he sneered. 'Congratulations! You're officially my owner. That's right—I'm Edward, your familiar cat spirit now.'

My mouth fell open, panic dribbling saliva onto my lower lip.

'No way! No bloody way!' I gasped. 'I didn't agree to this. Go back where you came from!'

I waved my hands in dismissal.

'Actually,' Edward frowned, 'you did agree. You know, you really ought to read the fine print in your contracts more carefully.'

He shrugged, a sardonic grin curling his lips.

'But... I can fill you in now that I'm here.'

I slumped back, exhausted, realising it must have been buried somewhere in my deal with the Satyr.

'Bloody hell,' I groaned.

Edward folded his furry little legs, clasped his hands behind his head, and beamed.

'Drive on, Watson.'

'Fine,' I growled. 'So, if you're my familiar, what do I get out of it? Three wishes? Unlimited wishes? Do you make coffee... polish shoes?'

Edward looked genuinely offended.

'I'm not your butler. But there are perks to having me, of course.'

He shrugged.

'You'll get the hang of it... along with the duties of looking after me, naturally.'

'Wait... I don't have to give you blood or something, do I?' I groaned.

'No, don't be ridiculous! I vastly prefer a bowl of cold milk... and don't go all Aladdin on me. I've got power, yes—but not that sort.'

I had so many questions, but I decided they could wait.

I sighed, turned the key in the ignition, and drove back towards Memphis.

'Fine,' I muttered. 'You can tell me everything on the way back.'

For the first time, Edward smiled without sarcasm.

Perhaps, after everything that had happened, that was exactly what we both needed.

A fresh start.

Jupiter

A Note to the Reader

If you've reached this page, thank you.

Every book is a conversation between two people who may never meet: the one who writes, and the one who reads. I'm grateful that, for a little while, our paths crossed here.

From the beginning, I wanted **The Silent Dance of Stars** to exist as a physical book. Something to hold, revisit and, perhaps, leave quietly on a shelf until the right moment called you back to it. For me, stories have always belonged not only in words, but in paper, ink and the simple act of turning a page.

The illustrations that follow are the tarot cards that open each part of the novel. They were created alongside the story, each one serving as a threshold into the chapters that follow while also standing as a piece of artwork in its own right.

If you have a moment, linger with them. Like the story itself, they aren't intended to explain everything. They are invitations rather than answers.

Some of the original artworks are also available as museum-quality Giclée prints through Ciro Correia Studio for readers who would like to bring a small piece of this world into their own.

Thank you for reading, and for spending time in this corner of the Studio.

Until our paths cross again.

— Ciro Correia

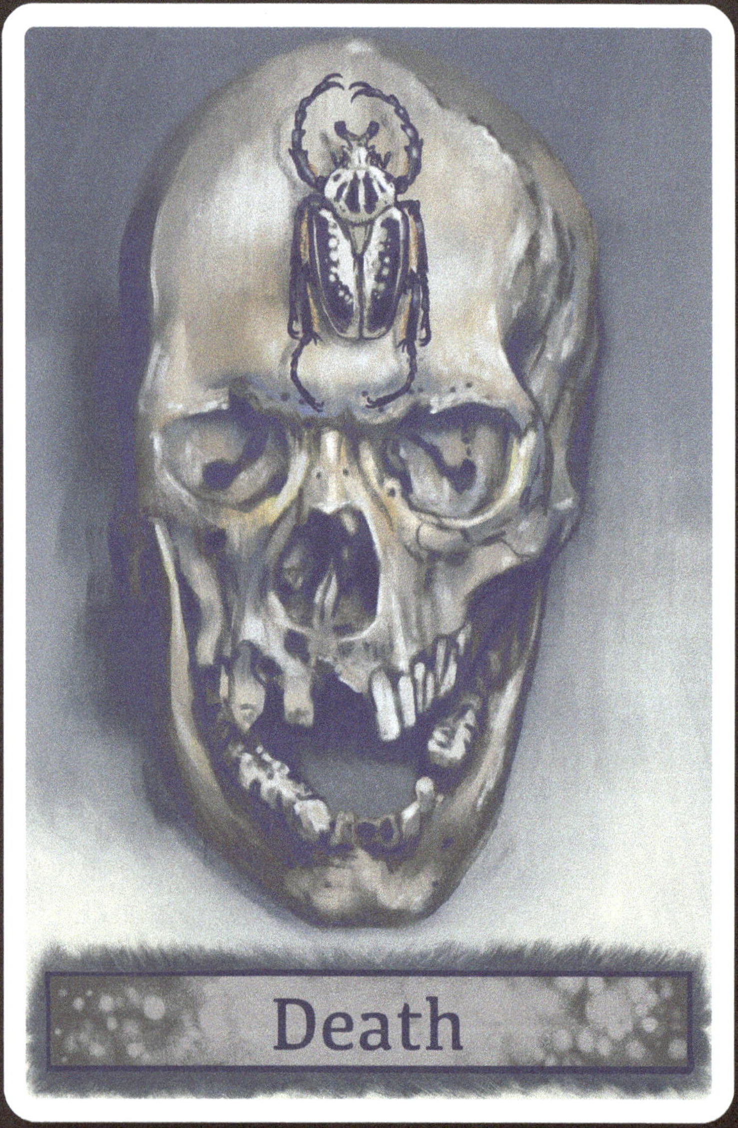
Death

The Lovers

The Fool

The Jackal

The Star

The Magician

Justice

The World

The HangingMan

The High Priestess

Letter from the Artist: On The Sun

I've long been fascinated by symbolic art and the quiet language of the esoteric.

Symbols have a remarkable way of speaking where words often cannot. They invite us to pause, to wonder, and to discover meanings that are felt before they are understood.

That fascination has shaped much of my work. Rather than separating the ordinary from the mystical, I prefer to let them exist side by side, allowing the familiar to become quietly extraordinary.

My interpretation of **The Sun** follows that path.

Instead of the traditional radiant sun suspended above the landscape, I chose to depict a woman stepping from an inner world into an outer one. She is neither goddess nor allegory in any fixed sense, but a symbol of awakening. Her nudity is not intended as sensuality, but as honesty—a life stripped back to its essence, free from pretence.

To me, the inner world is the place of memory, intuition and imagination. The outer world is where those hidden things take shape and become visible. The figure exists between those two realms, crossing the threshold from one into the other.

Like the story you've just read, this image isn't asking to be solved.

It is simply an invitation to look a little longer.

Sometimes the most enduring symbols reveal themselves slowly, changing as we do.

— Ciro Correia

The Sun

The Devil

The Tower

Strength

The Moon

The Hermit

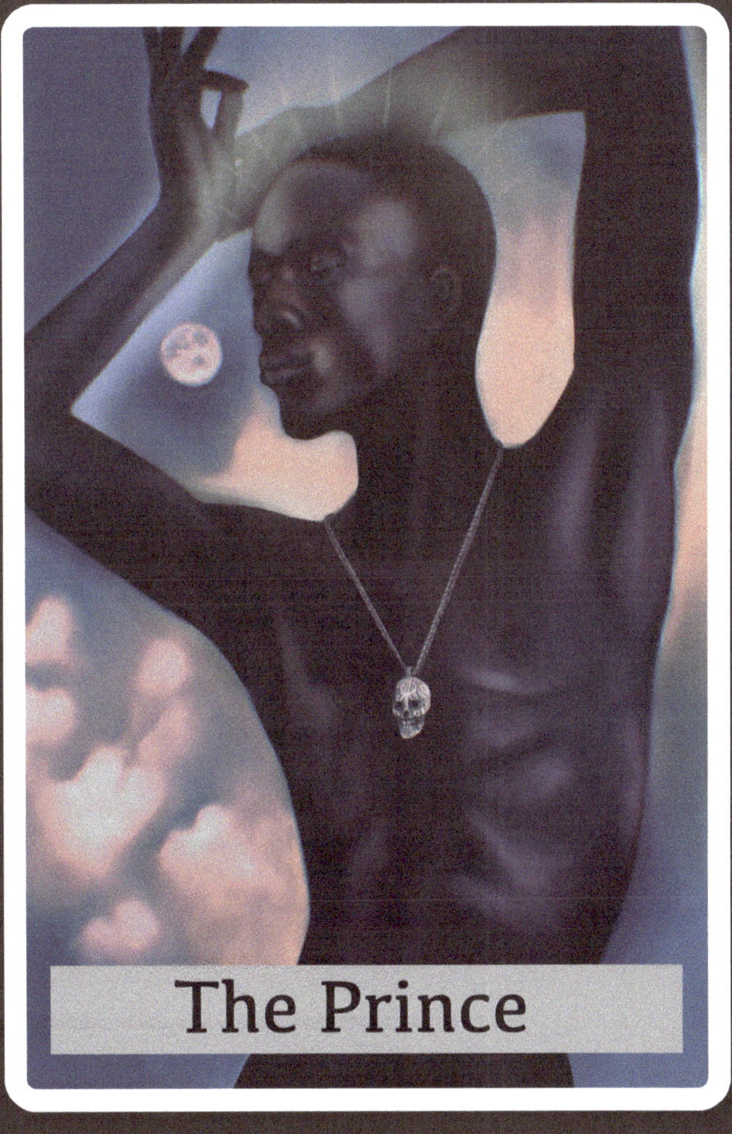
The Prince

About the author

Ciro Correia is an author, illustrator and designer based in Chichester, England.

Born in Angola, raised in South Africa, and now living in the United Kingdom, his work is shaped by a lifelong fascination with storytelling, symbolism and the quiet mysteries that lie just beneath everyday life.

When he isn't writing or drawing, you'll usually find him reading, walking, or enjoying a good cup of coffee while searching for the next story.

About Ciro Correia Studio

Ciro Correia Studio is an independent story studio dedicated to creating original worlds through novels, illustration and visual storytelling.

Its guiding principle is simple:

Stories come first.

Every project begins with a single question:

Does this serve the story?

The studio explores mythology, wonder, memory, hope and the quiet mysteries of being human, always with the belief that the most enduring stories leave readers seeing the world a little differently than they did before.

Because stories are more than entertainment.

They are invitations to imagine.

www.ingramcontent.com/pod-product-compliance
Lightning Source LLC
Chambersburg PA
CBHW040015120826
49724CB00019B/77/J
9781036964290